The cut felt deep.

The little bitch had punched her.

Despite the pain Ella bit down harder now, feeling oddly energized as more blood welled into her mouth. It tasted sharp and bitter, like acid.

Gaia had punched her. Her.

It *was* acid, she decided, stepping swiftly onto the third floor. Acid, pumping through her heart, coursing through her veins. She could feel it—couldn't she?—burning in her cheeks, raging in her ears. It would dissolve her. It *was* dissolving her. Eating her from the inside out. She had to hurry. There was no time to lose.

Ten feet down the hall to her dressing room.

Her gun was in the dressing room.

Don't miss any books in this thrilling series:

FEARLESS™

Available from POCKET PULSE

FEARLESS™

KISS

FRANCINE PASCAL

POCKET PULSE
New York   London   Toronto   Sydney   Singapore

To Nicole Pascal Johansson

An *Original* Publication *of* POCKET BOOKS

 POCKET PULSE, published by
Pocket Books, a division of Simon & Schuster, Inc.
1230 Avenue of the Americas, New York, NY 10020

 Produced by 17th Street Productions, Inc.
33 West 17th Street
New York, NY 10011

Copyright © 2000 by Francine Pascal

Cover art copyright © 2000 by 17th Street Productions, Inc.
Cover photography by St. Denis. Cover design by Russell Gordon

ISBN: 0-671-03945-8

First Pocket Pulse Paperback printing February 2000

10 9 8 7 6 5 4 3

Fearless™ is a trademark of Francine Pascal.
POCKET PULSE and colophon are trademarks of Simon & Schuster, Inc.

Printed in the U.S.A.

KISS

I'll probably never have kids. I'm not just saying that. There are a few really good reasons to think so:

1. I can't even manage to get a guy to kiss me, let alone . . . all that;

2. I seem to have very, very bad family karma (if you believe in karma, which I don't, but it's kind of a fun word to say);

3. Somebody tries to kill me at least once a week.

If you knew me at all, you'd know I'm not being a wiseass when I say that. Let me give you a quick example: I went on the first real date of my life recently, and the guy tried to murder me—literally—before the night was over. So, really, what are the chances I'm going to stick around on this earth long enough to find a guy to love me so much that I'd actually want to have kids with him in the far distant future?

But if by some miracle I ever

GAIA

did have kids, I would never, never, never have just one.

I remember this old neighbor of mine telling me how great it was to be an only child, how you got so much more support, love, attention, blah, blah, blah, blah. How you didn't have to share your clothes or fight over the bathroom.

I would die to have a sister or brother to share my clothes with. (Although to be honest, what self-respecting sibling would want any of my junk?) I fight over the bathroom with *myself* when I'm feeling really lonely.

The summer I was thirteen, the year after my mom . . . and everything, it was over a hundred degrees practically the entire month of August, so I used to go to this public swimming pool. All the lifeguards, and lifeguards-in-training, and lifeguards-in-training-in-training, and swim team members chattered and gossiped and giggled while I sat on the other side of the pool. I never made a single friend. One day I overheard my foster creature at the time say, "Doesn't it seem like all the other kids at this pool arrived in the same car?"

That, right there, is the story of my life. I feel like the whole rest of the world, with all their brothers and sisters and parents and grandparents and uncles and aunts, arrived in one big car.

I walked.

The neighbor I mentioned earlier, the one who was so psyched about only children? I think he neglected to consider how the whole scenario would look if you didn't have parents.

Gaia sucked in
a few shallow
gasps of air,
raised a pair
of wide,
haunted eyes
to his, and
whispered, "I
see dead
people. . . ."

the

color

of

fear

"MRS. TRAVESURA?"

At first Ella Niven didn't realize the voice was speaking to her. Then she remembered. *Travesura* was the Spanish word for "mischief." It was the name she'd given when she'd first made the appointment.

Flesh Crawler

She looked up from her magazine. The stunning Asian receptionist was smiling down at her. "The doctor will see you now."

Ella nodded. Setting down the magazine, she grabbed her purse and the shopping bag resting beside her chair and followed the woman.

There were several other women in the posh waiting room. All were reading magazines. All were the indeterminate age of the extremely wealthy—somewhere between thirty-five and death. Clearly most of them had consulted the plastic surgeon many times before this.

Ella noticed that most of the women also had shopping bags with them. She recognized the familiar logos of Chanel, Saks Fifth Avenue, Bergdorf Goodman, and a couple of other Fifth Avenue boutiques, all glimmering like badges of honor.

Ella's own shopping bag was from Tiffany. As she crossed the room, she was acutely aware of each of the other women taking note of the robin's egg blue bag in her hand.

The receptionist led her out of the waiting room and into a long, gray corridor. At first Ella thought the walls were made of slabs of marble—but was shocked to realize they were actually enlarged, black-and-white close-ups of human flesh. A gigantic palm here. A colossal kneecap there. She'd never considered how the wrinkles and creases of one's skin could look like striations in rock.

Up ahead, the corridor ended in a pair of brushed-aluminum doors. The receptionist indicated that Ella could continue on alone. When Ella was within a yard of the metal doors, they glided open soundlessly.

The office was large and spare. Floor-to-ceiling windows wrapped around two sides of the square chamber, giving a panoramic, sixty-story view stretching from Central Park to the East River.

As Ella entered, the doctor was standing behind a large, black desk that gleamed like highly polished onyx. Oddly, it was bare except for a light blue folder that seemed to float—weightlessly—above the slick surface. It must have been an optical trick.

The doctor was tall, and pale, and bald. He wasn't dressed in a physician's white coat, as Ella had expected. He wore a black suit over a black turtleneck.

Drawing closer, Ella discovered that her initial impression was wrong again. The man *wasn't* bald. His hair was white, but cropped exceptionally close to his skull. His skin was the same ghostly color. That's what had created the illusion of baldness.

Still, the doctor's eyes were his most remarkable feature. They were deep set and a light shade of yellowish green. They gleamed like cat's eyes beneath his brow. In all her life she had never seen eyes that color.

Not on a human, anyway.

"'Mrs. Travesura,' I presume?"

His tone of voice made it clear he knew it wasn't her real name.

She nodded cordially. "How do you do."

The doctor didn't answer but gestured to the chair opposite him—an artsy contrivance of chrome bars and black leather straps.

The doctor sat down. "I understand, from our initial conversation, that there is a certain . . . procedure . . . that you wish me to perform."

"That is correct."

"Now. If I am not mistaken, you are . . . shall we say, *employed* by a certain L—"

"Exactly," Ella interrupted. She needed to shut off this particular line of inquiry as quickly as possible. "I am. He, however, is not to be contacted under any circumstances. I must shield him from this undertaking. It is of utmost importance."

The doctor nodded, but he looked skeptical.

Ella knew he had past connections to Loki. That's

how she had found him. But if he were to contact Loki directly, Ella knew her plan would be derailed instantly. Loki would accuse her of deep, twisted jealousy. But the fact was, when Ella succeeded with this plan, and Tom Moore arrived at the bedside of his poor, disfigured, comatose daughter, Loki would be forced to give Ella the credit she was due.

For now, she needed to change the course of the conversation. She cast her gaze at the mysterious blue folder and gestured toward it.

It worked. "Ah . . . the portfolio," he explained, placing his hand lightly on the folder. "It represents my . . . *side business,* if you will. 'Before' and 'after' photographs of some of my more *interesting* accomplishments." He slid it across the desk toward her. "Care to take a look?"

Ella stared down at the ice blue folder in front of her, but she didn't touch it. She didn't need to see what was inside.

"Oh, c'mon . . . go ahead." He pushed the folder a few inches closer to her. "Aren't you in the least bit curious?" His tone was friendly. Flippant, almost. But—glancing back up at him—she saw that the man's eyes had locked on her with the cold, intense scrutiny of a snake. It was as if he were mentally willing her to look at the pictures. Daring her, even.

When she didn't respond, he reached forward and started lifting the cover. "Just take one little—"

"*I'm familiar with your work,*" she interrupted.

The doctor instantly snapped his hand away. The folder whispered shut.

He shrugged. "Suit yourself."

Ella had the feeling she'd just failed some kind of test. She tried to regain ground.

Sitting up taller, she leaned forward slightly, bowing her shoulders so that her cleavage was displayed at its most alluring angle. "Believe me, Doctor," she began in a persuasive voice, "I wouldn't be here if I weren't already *highly* confident about your . . . skills."

If the doctor noticed her breasts, he made no show of it. His eyes remained locked on her own.

"And yet," she went on—leaning forward a little more—"regardless of your expertise, I think you may find this particular . . . patient . . . to be an *extremely* unwilling subject."

"Many such patients *are* reluctant," the doctor agreed. "At first." His eyes seemed to sparkle at some dark, private memories.

"This one is different," Ella stated firmly. She was growing annoyed. Why wasn't he looking at her chest? She leaned forward even more. "You might as well know, Doctor: You're not the first . . . professional . . . I've contacted in this matter. Others have tried to treat this patient. They failed."

"My success rate is impeccable," the doctor assured her. "And as I informed you at the outset, Mrs.

Travesura, one gets what one pays for." He stressed this last phrase meaningfully.

Ella took the hint. Reaching down, she picked up the Tiffany shopping bag that was lying at her feet. She placed it on the desktop, sliding it toward the doctor across the slick surface. As she did so, her hand accidentally brushed up against the folder.

Despite herself, she flinched.

The doctor noticed this, and his lips curled in mild amusement. He took the Tiffany bag, glancing inside.

Ella watched him and waited. She didn't expect him to react at the sight of the money; he was no doubt used to seeing such large sums of cash. She was waiting for him to notice what *else* was in the light blue bag.

The doctor's smile faded. Reaching into the bag, he removed a small, rectangular device. It might have been a cellular phone, except that it had a tiny LCD monitor where the earpiece should be. He held it up, a question forming in his bile-green eyes.

"It's a tracking device," she explained before he could ask. "Satellite technology. Effective within a fifty-mile radius. It allows you to pinpoint the precise location of a radio transmitter." Opening her purse, she withdrew a tiny metallic chip about the size of an aspirin. "*This* transmitter, which will be planted on the subject tonight."

She paused to gauge the doctor's reaction. It was crucial that he go along with the plan.

"Interesting," was all he said. He placed the tracking device down on his desk and sat back in his chair, steepling his fingers together on his chest.

Keeping her voice steady, Ella continued: "You will use the device to track the subject. There is a telephone number on the back. Once you have completed the job, you are to go to the nearest pay phone and call this number. Is that understood?"

The doctor stared at her over his fingertips. "Perfectly."

Was he mocking her? She couldn't tell. But she didn't care now. This transaction was drawing to a close.

"Good," she said. "Well—uh, *Doctor*—I believe that about covers it."

She stood up. So did he. She would not let him try to shake her hand. The thought of being touched by those long, bloodless fingers made her flesh crawl.

There was only one more matter to square away before she could leave.

She placed her hands on his desk. "I have to make sure we're perfectly clear on one point," she informed him, trying to make her voice as threatening as possible. "You may be as . . . *thorough* . . . as you desire. In fact, I encourage you. But it is of the *utmost importance* that the subject makes it through the procedure. *Alive.*"

The doctor stepped around his desk, smiling widely and warmly. "Your concern, Mrs. Travesura, is quite touching," he said, his voice dripping with sarcasm. "But it's unnecessary."

He suddenly dropped his smile—and with it, his act. "The subject will live. I can assure you of that." His voice was much colder now. Deader. As devoid of life as his skin. "There's no challenge in it for me otherwise."

He nodded at the folder, still sitting on his desk. "*They* all lived," he informed her, his voice ringing with chilling pride.

GAIA MOORE MOVED QUICKLY ALONG

Shortcomings

West Fourth Street in the direction of Washington Square Park, not bothering to slow her pace for her friend, Ed Fargo, who wheeled along a yard or two behind her.

As she walked, Gaia switched the strap of her beat-up canvas messenger bag from her left shoulder to the right. It was a smooth, fluid movement—one she made often over the course of her day. If she was doomed to have the overdeveloped deltoids of a Russian gymnast, at least she'd make sure they were *equally* overdeveloped. Being a supermuscular freak was bad enough. Being a lopsided one was too much to bear.

Gaia was painfully self-conscious about her body. Even now she was aware of her muscular arms and shoulders, although they were safely camouflaged beneath the bulky yellow-green Polartec parka she'd started wearing since the weather turned cold.

Long ago she'd given up trying to fight it. No amount of doughnut scarfing could erase the six-pack definition of her abdominals. Her genetics were simply stacked against her. Her muscles were as much a part of her as her blue eyes and her light hair and her extreme devotion to chocolate.

"Jesus, Gaia, could you slow down? The speed limit is thirty miles an hour, last I checked."

Gaia cast a glance back at Ed. "Why don't you speed up? You've got *wheels,* for God's sake."

It was a game they played. If she'd actually slowed down for his benefit, Ed probably would have clocked her. He appreciated pity exactly as much as she did.

The chess tables were coming into view. Gaia hoped there would be a new face today so she could earn some money for lunch.

Over the past three months she'd developed a reputation among the chess players. When she'd first arrived on the scene, it had been fairly easy to score a twenty-dollar game. That was in late August. Now the only regular who would play her for cash was old man Zolov, an international master. Since Gaia had helped save Zolov's life back in September, the "undefeated chess champ" of Washington Square suddenly began losing to her at regular intervals. A little *too* regular. It seemed as if they'd traded the same twenty dollars back and forth ten times in the past week.

And then there was Sam Moon. Sam could also get a game off her, but he was a different story entirely. They had played only once. They played to a deadlock until she'd freaked out and forfeited her king. Sam wouldn't take her money, but he had walked off with her heart that day.

Impatiently Gaia gathered her long hair from where it blew in her eyes and mouth and threw it behind her back. She'd forgotten to bring a hair band.

Maybe if she were lucky, Zolov would let her win today.

If she were really lucky, Sam Moon wouldn't show up at all.

Ed had caught up and started badgering her the way he'd been doing all day. "Gaia. Do the line from the movie. *Pleeeease?*"

And maybe—if she were really, *really* lucky—a certain someone would get his wheelchair caught in a sewer grate any moment now.

She glanced in annoyance at her self-appointed best friend. What had she done to deserve him?

"I'm not going to do it, Ed. So you can stop asking."

"Please, Gaia? I'm going to Pennsylvania tonight, so I won't get to see you for a whole four days. Besides, I promise I won't laugh this time. I promise."

"That's what you said the last time. *And* the time before that." God, why had she ever attempted that stupid imitation? She was just fooling around in the cafeteria at school, and Ed acted like it was the most hilarious thing he'd ever seen in his life. He wouldn't shut up about it.

"That was the old me. I've changed since then. I swear."

"The only thing you've changed is your underwear—and that's debatable."

"*Guy-uhhhhhhhhh . . .*"

"Oh, sure, whine my name. That'll convince me."

"I'll pay you."

"You don't have enough money."

"Oh, you might be surprised."

"I doubt it. Seeing as you can't even afford socks that match." She gestured at his feet.

Ed shot her a confused look. "What are you talking about?"

"Your socks. Are you celebrating Christmas a month early? Or did you get dressed in the dark this morning?"

Gaia had walked a good ten paces before she realized Ed was no longer at her side. She spun around.

He'd stopped in the middle of the sidewalk and was bent over in his seat, staring down at his feet with a strange, aggravated expression on his face. "Aw, man. You're kidding me, right?"

Gaia put her hands on her hips. "Kidding you? You put them on, elf boy, not me."

Ed squinted up at her. "Great. Thanks. Make fun of the color-blind guy. Go ahead."

Gaia cocked her head. "You're not color-blind," she pronounced.

Ed frowned, crossing his arms. "I think I would be the one to know."

Gaia stared at him. Her hands slipped from her waist, flopping at her sides. "Seriously? You're color-blind?"

"Hey—don't worry. You can't catch it." Ed slapped his wheels, gliding toward her once more.

"It's just that you never told me."

"Hmmm, that's funny. It's usually one of the first things I say to people: 'Hi, I'm Ed. I'm color-blind.' I think it's good to get one's physical shortcomings out of the way, y'know, *up front*." He rolled to a stop in front of her feet, then peered furtively around the park. "Now, uh, Gaia, don't let this next bit of info freak you out, *but*..." He leaned in toward her, shielding his mouth with one hand conspiratorially. "... I'm *also* in a wheelchair."

Gaia was too busy looking at Ed's feet to think of a

good comeback. One green sock, one red. Could he really not tell them apart? Not at all? She raised her gaze to his eyes, studying them, not sure what she was looking for. They were a dark brown with gold lights. Eyes the color of a double espresso, she found herself thinking. Inwardly she groaned. *Guess you don't need those refrigerator magnets to write crappy poetry.* The point was, Ed's eyes didn't *look* color-blind. They looked . . . well . . . like regular, everyday eyes.

Regular, everyday, *annoyed* eyes.

"Please, by all means, Gaia. Keep staring at me like that. It does wonders for my self-esteem."

"Sorry—" Gaia barely had time to scoot out of the way as Ed blew past her. "It's just that you're the first . . . I mean, I never knew a person who was color-blind. What's it like for you?"

God, I must sound ridiculous, Gaia thought, stepping after him. Why don't I just say, Hey, Ed, you can't see colors, and I can't feel fear. Let's start a club!

Once she was beside him again, Ed looked up at her, amused. "Are you feeling okay, Gai?"

"Yeah. Why?"

"Because you asked me a question."

"And?"

"*And* . . . didn't you sort of stipulate way back when that we wouldn't ask each other questions because if *you* ask *me* something, that would mean *I* get to ask *you* something in return?"

This time it was Gaia who stopped in her tracks. "Right. You're right, Ed. Forget that I asked."

"No, no, no, no, no," Ed said, swiveling around to face her with a mischievous grin. "Not so fast. You can't back out now. A deal's a deal." He rubbed his hands together gleefully. "So—I believe the category is color blindness. What's the question gonna be?"

"Does it make you jealous?" She was startled to hear her own voice saying those words. She hadn't meant to say them out loud.

Ed blinked a couple of times. "Jealous?" he repeated, sounding confused. "What do you mean?"

Gaia chose her next words carefully. "Do you ever feel . . . upset . . . that other people can . . . experience something that you . . . can't?"

"Upset? Not really." He shrugged. "After all, it's not like being color-blind means everything looks black and white to me. I mean, I still see things in color. For example, I can tell that jacket of yours is the color of mucus. It's just that certain colors look alike to me. Mostly I have difficulty telling reds from greens." He pointed down at his feet. "Obviously."

Gaia self-consciously eyed her jacket. "Do you ever wish you *could* tell the difference?"

Ed nodded. "Well, sure. There was a pretty ugly incident involving hot sauce a few years back." He grimaced at the memory. "But most of those taste buds grew back. Eventually." He scratched the back of his neck. "Traffic lights pose a theoretical problem, but I figured out at a young age that red is on top, and green is on the bottom. Aside from that, I don't really think about it too much . . . except when I commit the very occasional fashion faux pas and some heartless person goes and points it out to me." He shot her a fake-hostile glance but quickly leavened it with another shrug. "But—honestly?—I can't say I'm jealous of people who aren't color-blind."

"Why's that?" Gaia prompted.

Ed bit his lip, thinking. "Hmmm . . . I can't explain it all that well, but it's sorta like this: I can't imagine a world with more colors than I see it in already. I just can't. And . . . well . . . I don't think you can truly be jealous of something if you can't imagine having it in the first place. Besides"—he ran a finger across the arm of his wheelchair, adding casually, almost to himself—"there are better things to be jealous of."

Gaia gave him a rare smile. What *had* she done to deserve him?

After a moment he looked away self-consciously. "Uh . . . did any of that make sense?"

She nodded. "Yeah. It did."

"Good." Ed sat up a little taller in his seat. "So, I believe now it's *my* turn to ask *you* something."

Gaia took a deep breath, then let it out slowly. "Shoot away." Part of her almost wished he *would* ask her one of her secrets. Considering all he'd witnessed over the past three months, she supposed it was a wonder he hadn't guessed them all already.

Ed stroked his chin thoughtfully, gazing skyward. "Let's see now. . . . I get to ask the mysterious Gaia Moore a question." He was clearly savoring the moment. "Anything I want. . . . Anything at—"

"You got five seconds, Ed."

"Okay, okay!" Ed scowled at her. Then he snapped his fingers. "Here's one: Where'd you learn how to—no, no, scratch that." He waved his hand in the air as if erasing an imaginary chalk mark. "I got a better one: Why don't you ever talk about your—" He stopped himself short again, reconsidering. "No, not that one, either. How about—"

Gaia let out a low grumble.

Ed looked up at her, as if he were just struck by an idea. "Say. Can I ask you to *do* something instead?"

Gaia cocked a wary eyebrow. This actually represented an easy way out, but she didn't want him to know it. "I suppose. . . ."

Ed grinned evilly. "Do the line from the movie."

"Except that."

Ed pointed at her with both hands. "Oh, no! You can't back out of it now. A deal's a deal."

Gaia glanced at her watch. "Wow, what do you know? It's already the end of lunch period."

21

"Gaia!"

She sighed, resigned. "Fine. But you better not laugh this time."

Ed pantomimed zippering his lip.

Gaia held up a warning finger. "I'm not kidding, Ed."

Now he crossed his heart, holding up three fingers in the Scout salute.

"All right." She moved a couple of steps to a nearby bench, plopping down on the hard, cold slats. Clearing her throat, she cast a wary eye around the immediate area. Aside from a cluster of `sooty-looking pigeons` pecking at the ground nearby, this particular section of the park was empty. Thank God.

Ed repositioned his wheelchair in front of her for a better view.

Gaia sucked in a few shallow gasps of air, gripped the neckline of her coat with two white-knuckled fists, raised a pair of wide, haunted eyes to his, and whispered, over a trembling lower lip: "*I see dead people. . . .*"

`Ed the Expressionless Eagle Scout` managed to maintain his deadpan for an entire second and a half. Then he let out a guffaw so loud, it echoed clear across the park, sending the pigeons exploding skyward in a frenzied, flapping cloud. It was a wonder he didn't flip himself over backward.

Gaia slapped her hands down on the bench, standing up in annoyance. "What's so funny? I thought I was pretty good that time."

"Good?" Ed was doubled over now, his face bright pink. "*Good?*" He could barely choke out the word through his laughter.

"Okay, that's it." Gaia kicked the side of his wheel with her boot and huffed off. "I'm outta here."

A few seconds later she could hear him behind her, struggling to catch her. "Gaia—wait—please—" All the laughing had left him panting for air. Good. She purposely picked up her pace. "Please—Gaia—wait up—I'm sorry—I'm sorry, but—it's just that—if you could *see* what you—"

She turned around. "Spit it out, Ed."

Ed placed a hand on his chest, taking a moment to catch his breath. "You have got to do the most terrible impression of being scared I have ever seen in my life."

He cracked up again.

Gaia hoped the sudden flush in her cheeks appeared to be a reaction to the cold.

Ed, my color-blind friend, you have no idea. . . .

I used to think you could pretty much divide people into two categories: those who believe in love at first sight and those who don't.

I was a proud member of the second category. I used to think you fell in love with your brain. . . . Um, that came out wrong. Let me rephrase. I used to think your brain was in use when you fell in love. You sort of decided it over time, like I did with Heather. I saw her, I thought, man, that girl is beautiful. I talked to her, I thought, yeah, and she's smart and funny, too. I spent some time with her and thought, hey, we actually like a lot of the same stuff. I kissed her and thought, yo, this is fun. After that, as far as my brain and I were concerned, we were in love.

Then I met Gaia Moore. Every time I've ever had anything to do with Gaia, my brain has said, shit, this girl is nothing but

pain, misery, and trouble. And in
this case my brain was totally
right. But in spite of my brain's
lack of cooperation, I've fallen
in love with her. It happened the
first time I ever saw her. It was
like a clap of thunder, a bolt of
lightning, a monsoon, all those
cheesy metaphors I never believed
before (although there actually
was a monsoon going on at the
time). There is no good reason
for me to love Gaia. There are
only good reasons against it.
Every day I struggle to release
myself from it. Every day I try
to convince myself that it will
go away.

So anyway, I guess you could
say my brain is sticking with the
second category, claiming that
no, there is no such thing as
love at first sight. My heart has
betrayed it in favor of the first
category, arguing, yes,
absolutely, it's the only kind of
love there is. And now my brain
and my heart aren't even on

speaking terms anymore. When I said "divide people," that wasn't exactly what I had in mind.

I told my friend Danny about this theory, and he told me he also had a theory for how to divide people: those who divide people into two and those who don't.

Her arms were
around him,
her
heartbreaking **hell**
scar pressed **hath**
against his
chest, her **no**
lips
against **fury...**
his ear . . .

"... AND MEDEA, SO CONSUMED

was she by her bitter jealousy, so desperate was she to take vengeance on her unfaithful husband, Jason, that she murdered her rival with a gift of a poisoned cloak and then went on to kill her own children...."

Heather Gannis glanced up at the animated face of her literature teacher, Mr. MacGregor, who was talking much louder than necessary and brandishing a paperback edition of Euripides. Jesus, why were parents so up in arms about violence on television? The seriously grisly stuff was happening in these Greek plays.

She heard a snort of laughter from the back of the room. She turned quickly, recognizing the laugh before seeing its owner. Ed Fargo, her former true love, was laughing at something Gaia Moore had written on the corner of his notebook. The sound of it was corrosive in her ears.

Gaia could make Ed laugh. It was a rare ability and another affront to add to the long list.

Heather wasn't superstitious. Unlike the ancient Greeks, she didn't believe in fate. She wasn't religious and had little tolerance for the wu-wu astrology and Ouija board crap many of her friends were into.

But for Gaia, she made an exception. Gaia, with her fairy-tale yellow hair and her long, graceful limbs, was too terrible to accept at face value. How could one girl captivate Heather's boyfriend, enslave her ex-boyfriend, humiliate her, nearly get her killed, and completely destroy her self-confidence in less than three months? Gaia was a clear message from Somebody Up There that Heather deserved punishment.

Since Gaia had arrived in September, her evil had radiated. First there were the slashings, culminating in Heather's own near death. Then there was the stuff that happened to Sam. Then Cassie Greenman. Heather, like the rest of the school, was haunted by her murder.

All these tragedies weren't a coincidence. They just weren't.

". . . So for Monday, I'd like you all to read *Oedipus Rex*." Mr. MacGregor wrapped up his lecture just as the bell rang, signaling the end of a very long day at Central Village High. "Have a great Thanksgiving holiday, folks."

The classroom burst into cusp-of-vacation activity. Heather sighed as she jotted the assignment in her notebook. She had a feeling that play was going to be another doozy.

"Hey, chick."

Heather glanced up as two of her friends, Carrie Longman and Melanie Young, materialized at her desk. "Hey," she said, digging around to find a smile. "Whatsup?"

"You feel like Ozzie's?" Melanie asked.

Heather carefully piled her books and zipped them into her backpack. Her eyes landed momentarily on her empty wallet. A large mochaccino at Ozzie's cost over three bucks. Her friends thought nothing of buying two of them a day. Heather couldn't keep up, and she refused to let anybody else buy one for her. The old Gannis pride kicked in triple strength when it came to shallow displays of fortune. Or lack thereof.

Besides, she had something important to do this afternoon. Something she'd put off for too long.

Heather stood and smoothed her long, slim, blood-colored skirt. She strode out of the classroom, and her friends followed close behind. "Can't make it. Sorry," she said breezily.

"Oh." Carrie hovered at Heather's locker, taking a moment to regroup. "How about Dean & Deluca? They have those excellent caramel brownies. We can go to Tower Records after and get started on Christmas shopping."

"You all go. Maybe I'll catch up later," Heather said noncommittally. "I've got something I need to take care of this afternoon."

Melanie and Carrie stared at her in silence, obviously hoping she would elaborate. She didn't feel like it. She slammed her locker shut. She pulled on her black nylon jacket and slung her backpack over her shoulder. "See ya. Leave your cell on, Carrie."

Once Heather was rid of them, she slipped into the

bathroom. She got weirdly obsessive about her appearance every time she was about to see Sam, although she knew her boyfriend was even more oblivious to her subtle efforts than most guys.

She studied her face and her hair. She applied a coat of lip gloss and ran a brush through her long, smooth hair. No perceivable difference. Staring at the high neck of her white T-shirt under her soft, black V-necked sweater, she suddenly had an idea. Ever since "the incident"—the slashing that had put her in the hospital late in September—she'd worn a scarf or a shirt or sweater with a high neck every time she left her apartment. Now she discarded her jacket, dropped her backpack on the floor, and pulled both the sweater and the T-shirt over her head at the same time. She pulled the two garments apart, folded the T-shirt neatly into her backpack, and put the sweater back on.

She spent another minute gazing at her reflection. Yes, that was a good idea.

SAM TIPPED BACK HIS HEAD AND

Choose rested it on the top of the park bench. He closed his eyes and soaked up the low, late autumn sun. For the end of November, the air was sweet and warm. Probably almost sixty degrees.

Wednesdays were his favorite days. His classes ended early, so he allowed himself to hang out at the chess tables. That was one of the great things about college—those one or two class days that left you lots of time to waste. He'd already hustled twenty bucks off an unwitting stranger, then given it right back to Zolov in a rout. It was a weird form of charity, but whatever. Hustle from the stupid and lose to the smart. 'Twas the season.

"Hey, handsome."

He lifted his head and blinked open his eyes. Heather was bearing down at twenty feet, beautiful as ever in her red skirt and whispery black jacket. He heard the dry acorns cracking under the heels of her boots.

"Hi," he said, rubbing his eyes. "How's your day?"

"Okay," she said. "The usual high school plundering of spirits. How 'bout you?"

He laughed. Heather was so cool, so together. Never awkward or at a loss for words. "Oh, you know. Wasting some more of my youth at the chess tables." He paused. "Looking forward to tomorrow."

Instantly he felt annoyed at himself for having gilded the truth like that. He was looking forward to the gauntlet of the Gannis family Thanksgiving in the very plain sense of the phrase—observing that it would take place in the near future. He wasn't looking forward as in eagerly anticipating it.

"Oh, yeah?" She angled her head coyly, causing a curtain of shiny chestnut hair to fall forward over her shoulder. It reminded him of sex, which started that tingly feeling spreading through his body, which in turn made him feel guilty about what had happened the last time they had sex. And the first time they had sex.

"Looking forward to my dad's dry, stringy turkey? My mom's sickly turnip-brown sugar thing?" she challenged. "Looking forward to Phoebe eating nothing and complaining about Binghamton? Lauren talking on her cell phone straight through dinner? Hmmm." She appraised him with one lifted eyebrow. "Are you telling me the truth?"

Sam laughed again, wishing his heart would listen to reason once in a while. "Well. *You'll* be there."

Heather awarded him a little smile. She pointed to the spot on the bench next to him. "Is this seat taken? Do you mind if I sit?" Her tone was light, but he registered that her eyes were serious.

He scooted over fast, feeling ungentlemanly. "Of course. Definitely. Sit."

She sat and dropped her backpack on the other side of her. She wasn't so close that any part of her was touching him, but neither was she so far that he couldn't feel her warmth. "Listen. There's something I need to talk to you about." She turned to face him, nailing him with her odd-colored eyes. They weren't blue, but they weren't not blue, either.

"Sure, of course." He was getting nervous now. He was saying "of course" too much. "Talk away."

"It's kind of serious. Just to give you fair warning. It's something we've been needing to talk about for a while now."

"Of c—" He clamped his mouth shut. He felt like strangling himself. "Okay. I'm warned."

Heather took a deep breath. "I know that you have some kind of . . . *relationship* with Gaia Moore."

Sam could tell it was painful to her to say the name, and he felt awful.

"I know that you know her somehow, and I need you to tell me what's going on between you."

Sam swallowed. Jesus, Heather had a knack for getting right to the point. He hoped his face didn't betray his dire discomfort. He needed to choose his words carefully. He cleared his throat. "There's nothing going on."

Liar. You think about her every hour of every day.

"I barely know her. I've hardly ever spoken with her. There's never been anything . . . romantic between us."

But you wish there were. You dream about her at night.

Sam glanced up, reminding himself that he was

having a conversation with Heather and not with himself.

"So what *is* there between you?" Heather pressed. "Why was she there the night we . . ." She trailed off and then started again. "How did she know you'd been kidnapped? Why did you need to leave in such a hurry the last time we were together in your room?"

All the saliva in Sam's mouth had dried up, and from what he could tell, it was never coming back. He tried swallowing again. "Honestly, Heather, I don't know. The last couple of months have been so strange. I really don't know anything about her." That last bit, finally, was a sincere answer.

"Have you ever . . . *been* with her?" Heather stopped and tried again. Here was a girl who accepted no cowardice, particularly not in herself. "Have you kissed her? Hooked up with her? Had sex with her?"

"No," Sam answered firmly. *But God, how I've wanted to.*

Heather looked relieved but no less serious. "Okay, here's the really important thing I need to say to you." She pulled one sleeve of her sweater up over the palm of her hand. "I don't like Gaia Moore. I hate her. I think she's dangerous, and I wish she'd stay away from you." Heather caught her breath for a second before she rushed on. She was nervous, but admirably determined. "I need you to tell me now that whatever there is between you is over. That you won't have anything

35

to do with her anymore." She fixed him with her eyes again. "Because if you can't, it's got to be over between you and me. You have to choose."

Whoa. Sam looked down at his jeans, pressing his hands into his thighs, raising his shoulders up around his ears. This was hard-core. This was much more than he'd ever expected. He had to think.

Heather was not only offering him a choice; she was offering him a way out. He could be free of the guilt and the craziness. He could be free to figure out what the hell *was* going on between him and Gaia.

"So is it over?" Heather asked, her voice quiet and wobbly.

Sam turned to her. The answer he'd been contemplating withered in his throat. Her eyes were round and glazed with tears. Her jacket had fallen open, and the low V neck of her sweater revealed a long, jagged rent in the delicate white skin along her collarbone. The cut through which she'd lost so much blood and nearly her life. It was still angry red in color. Still unhealed.

His mind flashed back to that night. Finding Heather in the park, lying in a puddle of her own blood. The strange, dissonant whirlpool of hospital sounds and smells and colors, then the unsettling piece of information that a girl from Heather's class, a girl named Gaia Moore, had seen the gang member with the knife in the park and she'd passed up an easy opportunity to warn Heather.

Sam's gaze was riveted on the wound. He couldn't seem to look away. All the while Heather kept her head up, seemingly unaware of what he was seeing and feeling.

"Sam?"

He dragged his eyes back up to her face. He was miserable. He was filled with shame. He was torn in two. "Heather, it's not only over. It never began."

Her arms were around him, her heartbreaking scar pressed against his chest, her lips against his ear by the time he realized that he hadn't said which girl he was talking about.

"Why are you like this?"

That is a question I've heard from a lot of adults in my life. Some of them related to me, some not. If they don't ask it outright, I see the question in their eyes. And I'm not being paranoid. Trust me.

"Like this" in my case means loud, impulsive, messed up, combative, undisciplined, annoying. Other stuff, too.

The reason the question gets asked so often, with such impatience, is because there's no easy explaining when it comes to me.

I come from a nice family. Two parents, not one. We're rich, not poor. We're well educated. Or I should say, they're well educated. They pay lots of attention to me. They read me books when I was little. They made me drink my milk. It's really not their fault.

I have two nice brothers. They both go to good colleges now.

Growing up, they only teased me
and beat me up the normal amount.

Why am I like this?

I don't know. Some people have
a lot of space between thinking
and saying or thinking and doing.
I don't have any. Some people
look at themselves from the outside and try really hard to make
what they see look good. I stay
on the inside. I'd rather feel
good than seem it.

Sometimes I love that about
myself. Sometimes I hate it.

Why am I like this?

I don't know. I have a couple
of theories, though.

It was not
of "utmost
importance"
that the . . . **like**
"subject" be
a
kept alive.
That had **woman**
been
scorned
their
mistake from
day one.

GAIA RESTED HER HEAD IN HER

hand, staring at what remained of her frozen pizza, trying to fight off a terrible wave of loneliness. It seemed mean-spirited of biology to have left fear out of her

Worse Than Stupid

DNA but to have made her feel loneliness so acutely.

The Nivens' brownstone was empty and quiet except for the odd siren or car alarm blasting from Bleecker Street. Those were sounds you stopped hearing when you lived in New York City. Like a buzzing refrigerator or the hum of an air conditioner. You incorporated them into your ears.

The kitchen was sparse and orderly as usual. There was no sign, other than her plate on the faux-country wooden table, that a seventeen-year-old girl had just prepared and eaten her dinner there. Gaia was camping at the Nivens' more than actually *living* there. Low-impact camping. After five years in foster homes she'd learned never to settle in too much, never to get comfortable.

George had been called away on business just before the Thanksgiving holiday. She liked George. He was awkward with her, but sweet and well meaning. He had known her father. She would even feel disappointed by his absence, but like the sirens on Bleecker

Street, disappointment was something so customary, Gaia hardly felt it anymore.

On the plus side, when George was gone, Ella was usually gone, too. And Ella was most nearly likable when she was gone.

Gaia washed her plate, dried it, and returned it to the cabinet. No trace.

Thanksgiving wasn't Gaia's favorite holiday. The day was designed around warm family get-togethers, parents, grandparents, uncles, aunts, cousins. Blitzing yourself on great food. Thinking about all the wonderful things your life had brought you and feeling grateful for it.

Gaia had no family anymore (save one recently discovered man claiming to be her uncle, whose name she didn't even know). On account of that, she had trouble feeling grateful. Instead it brought to mind the wonderful things that life had taken away from her, which sent her down the spiral of thanklessness. And that didn't require a special day. That was every day.

Gaia peered into the fridge. She was still hungry, craving something sweet.

Apparently George had done the shopping for Thanksgiving before he'd been called away. The refrigerator was crammed with food, including a massive raw turkey on the bottom shelf.

It was a little depressing, seeing all the food that George had bought and now wouldn't get to cook.

Depressing but not exactly tragic. Although George could find his way through a tuna casserole, Gaia suspected his culinary talents fell a few drumsticks short of turkey with all the trimmings.

Ella certainly wasn't going to do it. Gaia doubted George's dumb wife could figure out the recipe for ice. The only way Ella would put her hands in a turkey was if her Celine Dion CD had been shoved inside.

It was revolting how tightly Ella had George wrapped around her finger. For a person who made a living in the intelligence community, George Niven was pretty moronic when it came to matters in his own home. You didn't have to be in the CIA to see that Ella was playing him.

No, the only way that bird was getting cooked was if Gaia did it herself.

Without warning, Gaia's mind was flooded with a rush of overlapping images. Memories of another time, another place.

Chestnut stuffing . . . cranberry relish . . . a fire in a stone hearth . . . an ivory chess set, the pieces carved to look like Norse gods: Odin, Frigg, Thor, Loki . . . a man's sudden, shocked laughter: "My God, she just beat me, Kat!" . . . a gravy boat shaped like a swan and a woman's accented voice, saying: "It's lovely, isn't it? It was my grandmother's. Her name was Gaia, too. . . ."

The mental pictures evaporated at the sound of the

front door being unlocked, followed by the sharp, staccato click of high heels on the marble entranceway. The hall light snapped on.

Gaia glanced over at the wall clock. 9:51.

Great. Apparently Ella's coven decided to wrap things up early tonight.

Quickly Gaia reached across the counter and flicked off the light. She closed the refrigerator, not hungry anymore.

It was uncanny: No matter how hungry Gaia was, whenever Ella approached, appetite retreated. Maybe it was an allergic reaction to Ella's unique combination of silicone, hair spray, suffocating perfume, and spandex microminis.

With the refrigerator door closed, the kitchen was swallowed up in shadow. The only light now came from the hallway and the faint red glow cast by the microwave's digital display.

Gaia stood silently in the reddish gloom, mentally urging Ella to stay away from the kitchen. She was hoping to hit the park this evening, maybe see if she could lure a mugger or two. A run-in with Ella would put a damper on that plan. Ella would pull the Carol Brady routine, and Gaia was in no mood to answer stupid, pointless questions at ten o'clock at night. "How was school?" "Great! I purposely blew my history exam and scammed sixty bucks at the chess tables before dinner, and now I'm gonna go to the park to kick some punk ass clear into tomorrow. Thanks for asking!"

She had the sneaking feeling Ella would *not* be amused.

Gaia listened closely for signs of life, but all she could hear was the loud ticking of the grandfather clock in the hall. When Ella still hadn't appeared after sixty more ticks, Gaia stepped cautiously into the corridor.

Maybe this was her lucky night. Maybe Ella had gone upstairs already, sparing Gaia the scary sight of a grown woman who still looked to Barbie for fashion cues.

No such luck.

Ella was standing smack-dab in the middle of the foyer. True to form, she was sporting a metallic turquoise miniskirt with matching pumps, topped off with a fuzzy pink angora sweater that had probably been too tight on the baby she stole it off of.

Gaia's luck hadn't completely abandoned her: Ella was faced away from her and hadn't heard her approaching. Gaia could still avoid detection. In fact, she was all set to scurry back into the kitchen—until she saw what Ella was holding.

Avoiding detection suddenly stopped being important. "What do you think you're doing?"

Ella spun around, one hand still buried deep in the pocket of Gaia's electric yellow-green Polartec coat. For a second she just stood there—frozen, guilty—then she narrowed her eyes, jutting out her chin in defiance. "What does it look like? I'm searching for drugs." She started rifling through the pockets once again, as if daring Gaia to stop her.

Gaia was across the foyer in three swift strides. "Let me save you some trouble, Ella. There aren't any." Grabbing hold of her coat, she yanked it hard out of Ella's manicured clutches.

Ella reacted as if she'd been slapped, her hands recoiling like two wounded pink spiders.

Gaia stared her flatly in the eyes. "And for future reference? I don't do drugs." Then, just in case Ella still didn't understand, she added: "Leave my stuff alone."

Ella's nostrils flared. "You think I don't know what you do?" she accused. "You think I don't see you sneaking out of here at night, heading to the park? I know what goes on out there." She jabbed her finger at the front door, tossing her copper-colored hair indignantly.

Gaia rolled her eyes. "*Please.*" To Ella's blow-dried mind, the only reason Gaia might possibly want to go to Washington Square Park was to do drugs. Well, if that's what she wanted to believe, let her. There was no way Ella would buy the truth, even if Gaia had the patience to tell it to her. Which she didn't.

Besides, how did you explain that your hobbies

included luring out and beating up would-be felons for sport?

Hell, even someone with a measurable IQ would have a hard time believing that one.

Gaia turned to leave, but Ella suddenly seized her sharply by the arm, spinning her around.

"*I know what you are.*"

Ella's press-on nails felt like five plastic knives gouging through the flannel of Gaia's sleeve.

Gaia jerked out of the woman's grasp. "Trust me, Ella. You don't know the first thing about me."

Ella was physically shorter than Gaia, but her stiletto pumps put them at roughly the same eye level. Idly Gaia found herself wondering just what color Ella's eyes would appear to the color-blind Ed Fargo. To her they were the ugly, radioactive green of mint jelly. Did that mean they would look *red* to him? Or would Ella's *hair* look *green?* Somehow the mental image of a red-eyed, green-haired Ella wasn't too hard to conjure.

Ella's lips curled into a sneer. "I knew you'd be trouble the minute you set foot in this house. George wouldn't listen to me, of course. 'Poor little Gaia, she's had such a hard life. She needs our help.'"

Gaia was impressed. For a bimbo with no discernable skill as a photographer, Ella could do a pretty mean impression of her husband's voice. She'd obviously missed her calling in life.

Ella continued tauntingly: "Well, I got news for you. Maybe that wounded-bird routine works on George, but it never fooled me. Not for *one minute*." She punctuated the last two words with two sharp pokes to Gaia's shoulder.

Gaia glanced down at the spot where Ella had touched her. "Are you through?"

"Not quite. I also know you're doing everything in your power to flunk out of school."

Gaia raised an eyebrow. "Really?" *And what was your first clue, Nancy Drew? The string of* F*'s, maybe?*

"That's right. Your principal called to say that you're officially on academic probation." Ella smiled smugly. "Congratulations, Gaia. And after only three months. I hear at your last school, it took you a whole semester."

Whoa. This was definitely *not* the Carol Brady moment Gaia had anticipated five minutes ago. Gaia didn't know *what* role Ella thought she was playing tonight, but if the woman was hoping to get some kind of reaction from her, she'd have to keep on hoping. Gaia wasn't going to give her any satisfaction.

Ella crossed her arms and shook her head in mock pity. "Poor George. He still has some misguided notion that you're intelligent—that we'll actually get rid of you in a couple of years when you go to college. Ha!" She made an ugly snorting sound. "*That's* a joke. Do you think colleges would even *touch* a person with your grades? Do you?" Ella leaned forward, lowering her voice to a whisper. "Or do you think colleges simply let in little blond girls who can beat old drunks at chess and are friends with cripples?"

Gaia's hands involuntarily curled into fists. Her heartbeat accelerated. But she kept her voice remarkably cool and collected as she warned: "You should watch what you're saying, Ella."

"This is my house!"

Ella's voice exploded with such raw, unbridled rage that Gaia found herself backing away defensively. "In *my* house *I* say what *I* want *and you listen!*" Her breath was hot on Gaia's face.

My God, Gaia thought, who *is* this person? This wasn't the old Ella who Gaia knew and disliked. She had seen that Ella angry before, and it had never been anything even remotely close to this. *This* person . . . this was someone different. Someone wholly unfamiliar.

The woman's face was contorted in a mask of fury. Her pupils were mere pinpricks in two poisonous green irises. Her lips were curled away from her teeth.

"Things are going to change around here, *starting now!* From now on, you come straight home from school. No stops in the park, no chess games. *Understand?* You're going to go to your room and you're going to do your homework. No phone, no TV.

And at night you're going to stay in this house if I have to nail every damn window shut myself. You're going to stay in this house if I have to nail your *goddamn feet to the floor!*"

Whoever this person was—Ella or her more evil twin—Gaia had finally had enough.

"I don't have to take this from you," she informed the crazy woman standing before her. "You're not my mother."

"I'm *not?*" Ella reared back, slapping her left breast in a truly third-rate imitation of shocked dismay. "No, I suppose I'm not," she continued, leaning forward again, green eyes narrowing into slits. "*My* heart's still *beating.*"

`Gaia watched her fist smash into Ella's face before her brain even knew she was throwing the punch.` It was that automatic. That impulsive. As uncontrollable as a sneeze and (good thing for Ella) about as sloppy as one, too. Unlike her more thought-out punches, this one barely connected with its mark, catching the underside of the woman's jaw.

Not that it made a big difference.

Ella spun, crumpling to the marble floor like a sack of bricks, landing on her hands and knees.

Everything was suddenly deathly quiet.

For the next fifteen seconds there was nothing but the sound of Ella's steady, heavy breathing and the slow, rhythmic ticking of the grandfather clock in the hall: *Ticktock. Ticktock. Ticktock.*

Gaia felt like she should do something—*say* something—but she didn't know what. "Sorry" didn't seem right. For one thing, she wasn't sorry. Not yet, anyway. Maybe later she would be.

Instead she just stood there, frozen in place, absently rubbing the knuckles of her right hand, watching Ella's shoulders rise and fall, rise and fall, inside the tight angora sweater.

Ticktock. Ticktock. Ticktock.

After another fifteen seconds Ella slowly crawled away from Gaia toward the foot of the stairs. Once there, she reached up and grabbed hold of the banister, then hoisted herself to her feet. Her spandex skirt had bunched up around her waist, and she took a moment to pull it back down. She smoothed down her sweater. Then, squaring her shoulders, she started slowly up the stairs.

She was halfway to the second floor when Gaia found her voice.

"Ella . . ."

Above her, Ella paused but didn't turn around. Tilting her head slightly, like a sleepwalker hearing her name being called, she said softly: "Wait there." Her voice sounded strange. Thick.

She continued up the stairs.

Gaia watched as Ella's legs disappeared from view.

Listened as the click of Ella's heels faded away, drowned out by the clock in the hall.

Ticktock. Ticktock. Ticktock.

It sounded remarkably like a time bomb.

BLOOD. SHE WAS TASTING HER OWN

Dissolving

goddamn blood.

Once she was out of Gaia's sight, Ella moved more quickly. Around to the next flight of stairs. Eighteen steps to the third floor. Right foot, left foot, right foot. Up, up, up.

Her tongue felt too large for her mouth. It was too wide, too thick. As she mounted the stairs, she explored her tongue's surface with her teeth, wincing as her incisors sank into the gash she'd bitten into it when the little bitch had punched her.

When the little bitch had punched her.

The cut felt deep.

The little bitch had punched her.

Despite the pain she bit down harder now, feeling oddly energized as more blood welled into her mouth. It tasted sharp and bitter, like acid.

Punched her. Her.

It *was* acid, she decided, stepping swiftly onto the

53

third floor. Acid, pumping through her heart, coursing through her veins. She could feel it—couldn't she?—burning in her cheeks, raging in her ears. It would dissolve her. It *was* dissolving her. Eating her from the inside out. She had to hurry. There was no time to lose.

Ten feet down the hall to her dressing room.

Her gun was in the dressing room.

She didn't care what Loki would say. Didn't care what he would do.

She was tasting her own goddamn blood!

Besides, she knew what had to be done now. It was obvious.

Loki had been wrong. Loki *was* wrong.

It was *not* of "utmost importance" that the "subject" be kept alive. That had been their mistake from day one.

As long as his daughter was alive, Tom Moore wasn't going to risk her life by showing his face anywhere near her.

But the bastard *might* come to her funeral.

TICKTOCK. TICKTOCK. TICKTOCK.

Gaia stood in the foyer. Watching the stairs. Waiting for Ella to return.

Should she stay? Try to fix this gaping **Go!**

54

rupture? Was there any point? Could she make herself apologize for George's sake?

Stay or go?

Ella was insane. `This night was insane.`

Stay or go?

She could hear Ella's footsteps again. She was coming back down the stairs now, rounding the landing one floor above.

Without realizing she'd made a decision, Gaia let her long strides carry her down the hallway. Numbly she pulled on her coat and threw her bag over her shoulder. The cold doorknob filled her hand, and she turned it with a click.

"Good-bye, house. Good-bye, George," she whispered. "Sorry about this."

She had a feeling as she stepped out the door that she wouldn't be coming back.

I remember the summer I started carrying pennies.

I was five years old, and we were living in our Manhattan apartment. My mom's dad got sick late that spring. He was dying, it turns out. Every weekend when we'd drive my mother to visit him in his hospital in New Jersey, my dad would take me to the Jersey shore.

You see, when you're driving back into Manhattan from the Jersey side, you have to go through a tollbooth. Nowadays things are pretty high-tech, with laser scanners and special stickers you can get for your car, but back then my dad would pay using tokens.

Of course, to a five-year-old, a coin's a coin. And to me, those tokens looked just like pennies.

Somehow, in my little-kid brain, I concluded that in order to get back home, you needed pennies for the tolls. From that

moment on, I started carrying
extra pennies with me. Just in
case.

For some reason, I had this
silly notion that my parents
could somehow lose me. You know—
just take their eyes off me
around a corner or something and
not be able to find me again.
Maybe all kids think like that
when they're small. Anyway, I
wanted to make sure that if I
ever got separated from my
folks, I'd have enough money to
pay the toll and get back home
on my own.

Later on, when I was older and
knew better, I still carried pennies. By then it had just become
this sort of superstitious habit
of mine. My talisman. My good
luck charm.

It wasn't until I was in sixth
grade that my father finally noticed
and asked me about it. When I explained the whole tollbooth story to
him, he laughed. Told me I always
worried about the wrong things.

A year later my mother was
killed and my father took off,
leaving me behind.

So I guess it wasn't such a
silly notion after all.

I don't carry pennies for good
luck anymore. They don't work all
that well, as it turns out.

Mary attached
herself to Gaia
by the hand,
and Gaia let **a**
herself **reason**
be pulled **to**
toward a wait-
ing group that **stay**
for the moment
at least, could
pass as friends.

THERE WERE TIMES WHEN A

four-dollar vanilla latte
with an extra dollop of
foam seemed like the
answer to every single
one of life's problems.

Red Light, Green Light

Tonight it just seemed
like an overpriced cup of
coffee.

Sitting at one of the window seats at the Starbucks
on Astor Place, Gaia forced herself to take another slug
of the sickly sweet concoction. It wasn't easy. Ten minutes ago it had been lukewarm. Now it was closer to
cold. It reminded her of the milk left over from a bowl
of sugar cereal.

Outside, across Fourth Avenue, the giant clock face
on the side of the Carl Fischer building showed that it
was almost eleven.

God, what a night. Living with George and Ella
had never been great, but it was a place to be. A place
to keep what little stuff she had. And her tenuous toe-
hold in their house had made her a New Yorker. She
liked that.

Now it was gone, and she had that slightly
metallic, nauseating taste in her throat
that came with running away. Or drinking
syrup-sweet coffee soup. Or the combination.

She knew the taste because she'd run away before.

Never successfully, though. She always ended up back where she started or in a different foster home, facing even greater doubt and suspicion from her newest "family."

This time would be different. Packed into the various zippered compartments of her messenger bag and parka were bills totaling over eight hundred dollars—three months of chess winnings. She carried it on her all the time. It was ironic. She used to carry pennies for luck. Now she kept twenties for when her luck turned sour.

It was a lot of money, but it wouldn't last long in New York City. She would be smart to leave town.

With that thought, a picture bloomed in her mind. The face of Sam Moon, sitting across the chess table from her, drenched by rain, staring directly into her heart as no one, man or woman, ever had.

It would be hard to leave him. It would be crazy to stay for him.

Then there was Ed. Her first real friend since . . . forever. She was addicted to Ed.

And to the park. And the action. The density of criminals. The number of places where you could buy doughnuts at 2 A.M. The sirens.

But tonight Ed had taken off with his family to drive to Pennsylvania for a classic Thanksgiving with bickering parents and adoring grandparents. He wouldn't be back until Sunday. It just pointed out how different they really were. How different they would always be.

Sam belonged to somebody else (whom she incidentally hated). Ed was a decent, good person with a family who loved him. Far too decent for her.

There was nothing for her here.

She tipped her head and rested it against the cold glass window. The pale, late November color of her hands picked up a green glow from the traffic light at the intersection just beyond the window. Go.

Predictably, a minute later, her hands were bathed in red. Stop.

For minutes at a time she watched hypnotically as her hands changed from green to red.

Go. Stop.

Walk. Don't walk.

She'd let the traffic light decide her fate.

Behind her, there was a complaint of hinges and an inrush of street noise as someone pushed into the Starbucks through the side entrance. A second later Gaia was assaulted by a blast of arctic air. She felt its icy fingers snake around her neck and trickle down her spine and watched in morbid fascination as the skin of her arms pebbled into gooseflesh.

The sight transfixed her. It always did.

She traced a fingertip along the surface of her forearm—slowly, exploringly—from the crook of her elbow to her wrist. Every tiny, raised bump gave her a tiny, perverse thrill.

Gooseflesh. A symptom of fear.

Of course, in Gaia's case, it was just hair follicles reacting to an extreme change of temperature. That's all it would *ever* be with her. Still, she liked to believe that in some small, weird way, getting goose bumps was like getting a tiny glimpse into what fear felt like. The simple fact that she could experience one of fear's physical manifestations made her feel less . . . different, somehow. Less freakish. More . . . human.

The goose bumps were beginning to fade.

Gaia sighed. Who was she trying to kid? She would *never* know what fear was like. No more than Ed could know what it was like to tell red from green.

Red and green. Gaia suddenly remembered her appointment with Destiny. Would she stay or would she go? Taking a breath, she raised her eyes and looked out the window.

The light was yellow.

Gee, thanks, Destiny. You sure know how to toy with a girl's emo—

Gaia's thoughts were interrupted by something reflected in the plate glass window. Someone was rushing up behind her. Someone with red hair.

Before she could turn around, something cold and metallic was pressed against the back of her neck. "Don't make a move," a female voice warned.

Gaia didn't move. She just sat there, staring down at her arms.

There wasn't a single damn goose bump in sight.

MARY MOSS WAS EXPECTING THE

girl's shoulders to jump or at least her muscles to tense. They didn't, although Gaia did turn her head quickly. "Your money or your life," Mary growled, pressing the metal tube of lipstick into Gaia's back.

No Folks

Mary snarled menacingly, waiting for a reaction.

Gaia didn't look scared, but she didn't look quite tuned in, either. She was glowing red from a traffic light outside, and her eyes were wide and confused.

Mary softened her expression and produced the tube of lipstick for Gaia to see. "Gaia, it's me. Mary. Are you okay?"

Gaia seemed to pull her eyes into focus. She took the lipstick and examined it.

"It's called Bruise," Mary offered. "Great color, poor firearm."

Now Gaia was green. She handed the lipstick back.

"How's it going?" Mary asked, taking the seat across the little table from Gaia and tucking the lipstick tube in the outside pocket of her backpack.

Gaia looked pretty out of it. Her light hair was gathered in a messy wad at the back of her head. Her acid green jacket was half inside out, hanging untidily over the back of the chair, and her messenger bag was clamped between her feet on the floor. On the table before her was the better part of a once frothy coffee substance.

Gaia rubbed her eyes. "Sorry. You surprised me. I'm—I'm . . . all right. How 'bout you?" she answered vaguely.

Mary studied the girl's face, wondering what was really up, knowing she'd probably never know. That was part of what made Gaia fascinating to her.

"Great. I'm not going to sleep tonight," Mary announced.

Gaia was paying attention now. "Oh, yeah?"

"Yeah. The night before Thanksgiving is one of the great nights in New York. It's a night for locals."

Gaia looked puzzled. "As opposed to . . ."

"Tourists. Gawkers. The bridge-and-tunnel crowd. Hardly anything that New York is famous for is actually happening for the locals. Broadway shows. Carriage rides through Central Park. Those dumb theme restaurants. The stores on Columbus Avenue."

"Um. Okay," Gaia said, not caring enough to argue if she did happen to disagree.

"Obviously the parade tomorrow is a major gawk

fest. But tonight, right outside the park, they blow up the floats for the parade. That part is still fun. It doesn't really get good until after midnight, so I'm going to a club first to hear this very cool neighborhood band. You want to go?"

Gaia just looked at her, waiting for her to finish, clearly not feeling a big need to act friendly. That was another thing Mary liked about her. "Well. Thanks and all," Gaia said distractedly, tapping her fingers against the table. "But—"

"You have other plans," Mary finished for her.

Gaia cocked her head. "It's not that. It's—"

"So come," Mary said.

Still there was hesitation in Gaia's face.

"You've got a curfew?" Mary tried.

Gaia shook her head.

"Your folks wouldn't be into it?" Mary suggested.

Gaia shook her head. "No folks."

"No folks?"

"I don't have any," Gaia said. Just a statement of fact.

"Jesus. I wasn't expecting that answer. God. Sorry."

Gaia's eyebrows collided over her nose. She was angry. "Sorry for asking me a perfectly normal question? Why do people say that? Why do they always flip out and apologize for no reason?" Her eyes were intense, challenging.

Mary's own anger reared up instantly. "I'm not

sorry I asked you the question, you idiot," she snapped. "I'm sorry your parents are dead."

Gaia's eyes widened, then her face got calm. "Oh."

"Fine," Mary said. She got up to order a triple espresso from the lone counter person. Starbucks sucked, but her favorite café had just changed management and installed computers every five feet. She turned back to Gaia, pleased to see the girl had gotten over her anger just as quickly as Mary had. "So, you coming?"

Gaia looked somewhat bamboozled. "I guess. Sure."

"... I'M BLIND. I'M EMPTY. I'M

stupid. I'm wrong...."

Just Like Sam

Gaia wasn't quite sure how this had happened.

She'd gone from being a bleak New York casualty, a teenage runaway, to being a frivolous club kid. Here she was, sitting in a round, red velvet booth at a downtown club surrounded by New York's young indulgents, listening to a band, Fearless, whose name and lyrics dogged her life in the creepiest way.

". . . I need you to tell me I'm not what I am. . . ."

The singer was ranting. Gaia stared into her vodka and tonic and tried not to think about it too much.

Most of the people at the table, including Mary, were on their third drinks before Gaia had drunk a third of her first. She didn't like alcohol very much. For one thing, it didn't taste good. Maybe that was babyish of her, but it was true. Besides, from what she could tell, the real reason people drank was to dull their fear. Not what Gaia needed. What if alcohol consumption pushed her from zero fear into negative fear? Gaia slid the sweaty glass a few inches toward the center of the table. That didn't seem like a good idea.

She turned her head as Mary tugged on a piece of her hair and then glided toward the dance floor. "You're having fun," Mary shouted over the din. It was more command than question. "Want to dance with us?"

"No," Gaia mouthed. It did actually look like fun, but somehow it didn't seem right, punching Ella out cold and hitting the dance floor in the same two-hour period. She felt obligated to remain dysfunctional and sullen for at least another hour.

Still, she couldn't help smiling at Mary, who was whirling like a dervish through the crowds. Mary was a wild dancer, not surprisingly, and her hair paid no attention to gravity. Gaia couldn't help admiring her. Mary had none of the self-consciousness that sometimes made it embarrassing to watch a person dance.

Gaia glanced at her watch. If she was leaving town, she needed to get going. Traveling on Thanksgiving was notoriously bad. It would be smarter to catch a train or a bus tonight. That way she could sleep in transit and not have to pay for a place to stay.

All of Mary's friends were dancing now. Gaia was alone in the booth. The place was packed, and she felt a bit self-conscious taking up this seating area for eight. She realized a guy standing by the bar was looking at her. No, make that staring. He appeared to be at least thirty. Ick.

Oh, shit, he was coming toward her. She directed an intensely unfriendly expression at him. *Go away now. I do not like you.*

He turned back to the bar. Ahhh. Good. Gaia had to hand it to herself. She could give a mean look like nobody.

Gaia gazed around the club. She'd never been to a place like this before. It was loud. It was dark. People were having fun. It seemed like a great place to go if you were a bored New York City kid looking to hook up. It was a weird place to go shortly after you'd decked your so-called foster mother, on a night you were running away for good.

But what if she *were* just a regular kid, stressed out

and angst ridden in a contained, urbane, happy kind of way, looking to hook up? It was a fun game to play sometimes.

She scanned the bar. There was a guy near the front windows who was sort of cute. He had hair the same color as Sam's. His nose and chin couldn't compare, though. And he appeared to be at least five inches shorter than Sam.

Another guy in a booth two away from hers had a good smile. Nice teeth. A little crooked. His eyes were nice, too. Not like Sam's, of course. Not turn-your-world-over nice. Besides, he was wearing one of those big, fancy metal watches. She hated those.

She slid her drink around in its little puddle on the glass table. The volume in the place notched up even higher. She turned to the entrance and saw another cluster of people packing themselves in. Her eyes froze. Oh, wow. There. That guy was beautiful, Gaia thought distantly. Tall, perfectly built. He had gorgeous red-brown-blond hair, neither wavy nor curly but somewhere in between. Just like Sam, her mind informed her dreamily.

Holy shit. Gaia sat up very straight. He wasn't *like* Sam. He *was* Sam. Her mind raced. Her heartbeat quickened. Goose bumps sprouted on her arms. *Almost like fear.* But not fear. Something else.

Gaia's eyes darted to the faces of Sam's nearest companions.

Clunk. Down slid her hopes.

Yes, indeed. The good-news, bad-news duo. Hateful Heather was in her usual spot right there beside him. Why *shouldn't* Sam and Heather make an appearance on this night from hell? How could it be otherwise?

Gaia averted her gaze. She pointed her face at the tabletop. She really didn't want them to see her. A word from Heather might just throw her over the edge.

Suddenly she felt terribly conspicuous in the booth by herself. Where were Mary and all her friends? Why couldn't they park their damn butts in the booth for five minutes and stop having so much fun? Grrrr.

Gaia rested her face in her hand, using her fingers to cover up almost the entire part of her face that Sam and Heather could feasibly see from their angle. She would just stay like that until they got busy dancing or went to the back, and then she'd leave. She'd head for the bus station. Fine.

Oh, no. She couldn't actually look up to confirm her suspicion, but she had a terrible feeling that the group, which included her favorite couple, was heading straight toward her booth. There was definitely a shadow moving in. No. Go! Go!

"Excuse me? Would you mind if we shared your booth?" It wasn't a voice she recognized. Could she get away with not looking up?

"Excuse me!"

Go away, she urged silently.

"Excuse me!"

All right, that was annoying. She snapped her head up just as Heather and Sam registered the reality of whom they were about to share a booth with.

Who looked least happy? Sam? Heather? Gaia?

Hard to say.

Gaia thought she gave a mean look, but Heather's was better.

Gaia shot to her feet. "All yours. I was just going."

Six pairs of eyes stuck on Gaia as she fumbled to put on her parka. It seemed to take two hours. First it was inside out. Then she couldn't get her hand through the sleeve. As she grabbed for her bag, she knocked over her drink and spritzed the group with watery vodka and dead tonic. Why couldn't she keep her beverages to herself?

She couldn't bring herself to look at Sam. This wasn't happening.

"Gaia, wait." It was Mary, suddenly positioning herself as a bulwark between Gaia and the booth stealers. "Where are you going?"

"I—I gotta go. Now."

Mary looked around. She took in the presence of Heather. A light dawned in her eyes. "Hey, if it isn't the charming Ms. Gannis. Gosh, I remember the last time we were all at a party together. You were riding quite the welcome wagon that night."

Heather was silent.

Mary gave Gaia a confident smile and spoke loudly enough for Heather's benefit. "Don't worry, Gaia. If Heather treats you like that again, I'll smack her."

Heather looked stunned. A couple of Heather's friends seemed to think Mary was kidding around. Gaia didn't look at Sam to gauge his reaction.

Mary attached herself to Gaia by the hand, and Gaia let herself be pulled toward a waiting group that, for the moment at least, could pass as friends.

"Bitch," Mary mumbled to Gaia, not letting go of her hand. "Let's get out of here."

Gaia felt like crying as she bobbed along after Mary. Nobody ever took care of her like that. Gaia was so taken aback, she didn't know how to feel.

Following the electrified red hair, she experienced a rush of real warmth in spite of the stiff, late-autumn breeze.

Maybe there *was* a reason to stay in New York for a while longer.

HEATHER FELT LIKE SHE WAS CHEWING

Poison

on a lemon. She couldn't seem to get the sour taste out of her mouth or remove the pinched expression from her face.

Sam sat down next to her, stiff as a two-by-four, saying nothing.

That was the best strategy. They would just let this pass and get on with their night. No need to talk about it.

"Who is that girl?" Sam's friend Christian Pavel wanted to know.

"You mean Mary Moss? The redhead?" Heather heard her friend Jonathan Singer respond.

"No, the blond one."

Heather waited numbly for the conversation to be over. She tried to think of some effective way to change tracks.

"That's Gaia Moore," Jonathan said flatly.

"She's unbelievable," Christian said.

Every person at the table waited in uncomfortable suspense to hear the precise way in which Christian Pavel found Gaia Moore unbelievable.

"She's gorgeous. A total goddess. Do you know her? Can you introduce me?"

No one said a word. Heather's mouth was drawn up like a twist tie. She felt like crushing all ten of Christian's toes under the table.

Sam cleared his throat. "H-H-Have you all seen this band before?" he asked the group gallantly, putting a wooden arm around Heather's shoulders.

Conversation resumed. Heather watched Gaia's back disappear through the door. She wished she could give Gaia a poisonous cloak.

Then again, Gaia's phlegm-colored jacket was pretty poisonous as it was.

SAM SAT IN THE BOOTH, AS CROSS

Lustful Looks

and sullen as a sleep-deprived toddler. Too sullen to drink. Or dance. Or make small talk.

He was annoyed at Heather for being his girlfriend. He was annoyed at Christian for looking lustfully at Gaia. (That was *his* department.) He was annoyed at Gaia for a whole list of things:

1. Not being his girlfriend;
2. Looking so spectacularly beautiful;
3. Ruining his life;
4. Ruining his relationship;
5. Not meeting his eyes for a single second tonight;
6. Not being his girlfriend.

Mostly he was annoyed at himself. For blundering deeper into the thing with Heather. For being so goddamned stiff and awkward tonight. For not talking honestly with Heather about what was really going on. For having blown a perfectly good chance to do so.

For still staring at the door fully forty-five minutes after Gaia had walked through it.

My Dear Gaia,

Having seen you so recently (though you did not see me), my pain at being apart from you is only stronger. You have grown into a formidable woman, Gaia, as your mother and I knew you would. Your strength and intensity still astound me. I see now that you have the spirit to fight fiercely for your life, and that is a great comfort to me.

My other comfort is the knowledge that at last you have a good home with my kind old friend George. It's a safe place. I trust George will do his very best by you. I'm glad to know you'll have Thanksgiving there, with someone who truly cares for you.

Each year at Thanksgiving, I write to tell you that you are my reason for thanks, my reason for living. Each year, with my heart full of hope, I pray that next year we'll spend this holiday together. And though realism chips away at my hope, I'm still praying.

Know that I love you, Gaia. That you are always in my heart.

Tom Moore signed the letter and thought about Katia. Twice a year he allowed himself to cry for her, and this was one of those times.

When he was done, he walked to the file cabinet.

The top drawer was stuffed full of letters like this one. He found the manila folder labeled Thanksgiving Letters and dropped it in.

He dug his hand in the pocket of his corduroy trousers and felt the penny that lay in the bottom. Perhaps, with luck, this would be the last time he would need to write to Gaia on Thanksgiving.

Gaia clutched the stretchy plastic in her fist as they rose under a cloud of helium, higher and higher.

fun, for a change

"WHAT *THE DEVIL* WENT ON THERE tonight?" Loki's voice thundered.

Ella stood before him, heavy with a strange mixture of shame, pride, and frustration. Her jaw throbbed, and her tongue felt like it belonged to somebody else. "We fought.

The Good Uncle

She punched me. She left." Ella didn't bother to mention the part where she got out her gun and went after Gaia, fully intending to blow her brains out. Luckily that part didn't appear on the surveillance tape.

"Stupid woman, have you lost your mind?"

Ella cupped her jaw tenderly. There would be no sympathy from him. That was certain. "The girl hit me."

"I would have hit you, too, the way you carried on," Loki said sharply.

Ella held her painful tongue. It was as expected.

"Absurd self-indulgence," he spat, pacing across the soft, honey-colored herringbone floorboards. Last month he had a vast loft above the Hudson River. Tonight she'd been ordered to meet him in a starkly modern apartment building on Central Park South. He'd only be there so long as he kept perfect anonymity. Then he'd relocate again. "Why I put up with you, I do not know."

Ella remained quiet. He'd get bored of the tirade eventually. The greatest mistake would be to attempt to defend herself. That would only inject a surge of energy into the project. Where Loki was concerned, what the world gained in a terrorist, it had lost in a lawyer.

His angry voice faded into a dull roar. Ella stared out the large picture windows, waiting for him to be done. Three-quarters of a mile uptown, the enormous helium balloons for the Thanksgiving Day parade were rising to life from the lawns of the Museum of Natural History on Seventy-seventh Street. Long ago, in her other life, she'd gone with friends to watch.

That was before Ella had been "discovered." Well before Gaia had come into their lives, a much more perfect fulfillment of Ella's early promise. Ella felt a wave of nausea climbing her chest.

"Ella!"

She turned to him. Oh. He was finished, then. He'd asked her a question of the nonrhetorical variety. "I'm sorry?"

"You are sorry. A truly sorry creature. I asked you why you were caught with your arm in Gaia's coat."

"I was planting the tracking device," Ella replied.

"And were you able to complete that *onerous* task?" His voice was laced with sarcasm.

"I was."

"Fine. And I gather you've chosen someone to perform the job?"

"Yes." Ella fiercely hoped he would not ask who that was.

"Well, then. With any luck we'll be done with Tom shortly." He smiled the least cheerful smile Ella had ever witnessed. "That should be fun. And then the real plans begin."

"SO WHO DO YOU LIKE?" MARY asked. "Clifford, the big red dog? Random Rugrat? Snoopy?"

The night was misty. The stones around the beautiful, castlelike Museum of Natural History were slick with yellow and brown leaves. Gaia and Mary  were still clutching hands like kindergarten friends, running through the crowds, watching the enormous balloons come to life. They'd left Mary's friends to their club hopping half an hour before.

"Spiderman is cool," Gaia observed, gazing at the balloon reaching four stories into the sky. A net above them kept the balloons on good behavior until the parade began in the morning.

"Spiderman is already up, up, and away," Mary said somewhat breathlessly, pulling Gaia along. "We need to pick one that's only partway blown up."

"We do?" Gaia asked.

Mary raised her eyebrows mischievously. "We do."

Gaia caught up even with her. "What exactly are you planning?"

"Something fun. You'll see." She glanced over at Gaia. "You scared?"

"Uh-uh," Gaia replied.

"Here." Mary yanked her to a stop. "These ones are good. Shhh. Stay still a minute."

The ones Mary was referring to were huge ponds of half-inflated plastic, one red, the other green. Gaia couldn't tell what they were.

Mary looked around. "Okay, follow me. Move quickly, before anybody sees us."

Gaia nodded, intensely curious.

Mary paused in thought. "Hang on. Which one? Red or green?"

"I don't care," Gaia said.

"Pick!" Mary ordered.

Gaia rolled her eyes. "They're the same. It doesn't matter. I don't even know what we're doing."

Mary was still glaring at her expectantly.

"All right, fine. Red," Gaia said.

"Go," Mary hissed.

She darted around the growing balloon to the side

that was closest to the museum fence and used the fence for a boost. She transferred her weight from the fence to the balloon, clamored up the soft, loose plastic, then rolled down into the sagging middle. Gaia followed close behind. When they settled in the middle, they had to cling to the plastic to keep from rolling on top of each other.

"This is cozy," Mary said, laughter in her voice.

"I still don't know what we're doing," Gaia said.

"Shhh. Stay still. We have to keep quiet."

Mary's excitement was contagious. "Why?" Gaia asked.

"'Cause the last time I did this, I got arrested," Mary explained happily.

"Oh," Gaia said.

"Scared yet?" Mary asked.

"Not yet," Gaia replied.

Gaia heard the rush of helium into the balloon get louder.

"Cool," Mary whispered. "They're turning it up."

"They?"

"The inflators," Mary said.

"Is that a word?" Gaia asked.

Mary's giggle came out like a snort. "I think so."

Gaia felt the helium filling the space under them. They were rising appreciably. "Now what?" she whispered.

"We wait," Mary said. She reached for Gaia's hand and held it again. Gaia was so unaccustomed to physical contact (apart from punching people) that it felt weird to her. Weird, but nice, too.

As the minutes passed, the plastic began to fill and grow around them. Soon the thin, rubbery plastic was puffing up all around them, becoming more and more taut.

"What is this balloon, anyway?" Gaia asked.

Mary lifted her head and looked behind her. "Judging from the green one next door, I think it's an M&M."

"An M&M?"

"Yeah, look." Mary rolled partly onto her side and pointed at the green twin.

"We're on a giant red M&M?" Gaia realized she was getting punchy because for some reason, this seemed hilarious.

"Okay. This is where it starts to get fun." Mary's face was flushed with anticipation. "Hold on tight, okay? I think we've got a facial feature of some kind here."

It was thrilling. Gaia clutched the stretchy plastic in her fist as they rose under a cloud of helium, higher and higher. She was amazed nobody had seen them yet. She twisted her head and saw the buildings above. The ritzy apartment buildings on one side, the museum on the other. They were rising faster now, above the streetlights, nearing the tops of the trees.

Closer and closer to the gauzy, dark purple night sky. She looked ahead to the ever improving view of Central Park with its dark carpet of trees and the twinkly lights along Fifth Avenue.

Gaia felt her own breath swelling inside her chest. It was magical. "Beautiful," she whispered to Mary.

Mary squeezed her hand.

Gaia tried to stamp this feeling, these sights, into her brain so she could remember them later, when she needed to convince herself there was happiness in the world.

"Oh, shit!" Mary suddenly cried, puncturing Gaia's reverie. Mary yanked her hand from Gaia's, pinching wildly at the plastic of the balloon to steady herself. "I'm losing it, Gaia!"

The plastic had grown so taut under their hands, it was hard to keep holding. Mary's grip was slipping fast.

Gaia turned to her new friend, expecting to see fear in the girl's eyes. Instead she saw wide-eyed thrill.

"Gaiaaaa!" Mary was yelling. "Eeeeeee! This is where it gets *really* fun! When I say go, let go!"

A laugh erupted from Gaia's throat. This was crazy. It *was* fun.

"Go!" Mary screamed.

"Ahhhhhhhhh!" The two girls' voices mingled in a

scream as they slid on their stomachs all the way down the growing mountain of balloon and landed hard on the ground.

They lay there for a moment in a tangled clump.

"Are you okay?" Mary asked, pushing her hair out of her face, trying to organize her limbs.

"Okay? That was awesome!" Gaia jumped to her feet and pulled her friend beside her. "Let's do it again."

Mary laughed and swatted Gaia on the shoulder. "I *knew* we were gonna get along."

TWO HOURS LATER GAIA LAY BESIDE

Mary on the grassy part of Strawberry Fields and watched the first light of sun spread across the sky. The air felt damp and surprisingly mild.

Gaia fell in love with the place on first sight. She loved the curving pathways and the odd accumulation of humanity gathered on the handsome benches. She loved the white-and-black mosaic that said "Imagine" in the middle.

"This is my favorite place," Mary said, grabbing the sentiment right from Gaia's mind.

"I see why." Gaia turned her head to see Mary's face.

Mary yawned and raised her arms, stretching long fingers toward the sky. Gaia caught the yawn from her.

"Hey, Mary?"

"Yeah."

"Thanks for inviting me along on this night. It's been great."

Mary turned to her and smiled. "It wouldn't have been great without you."

Gaia must have been very tired because she was saying things she would never normally say. She was forgetting to censor her feelings and words, forgetting what the consequences could be. "And thanks a lot for looking after me at that bar."

"No prob," Mary said to the sky. "I always take care of my friends."

Gaia thought for a few moments. "Why is that?" she asked. Her voice was so quiet, she wasn't sure it would carry to Mary, two feet away.

Mary yawned again. She put her fingers into her fiery hair. "Because I can afford to."

Gaia squinted at her. "What do you mean?"

"I get a lot of love. From my folks, my brothers. I have extra."

In the pale morning light, that seemed to Gaia both a totally unexpected and beautiful thing to say. She tried to imagine what kind of parents would love Mary so well *and* let her stay out all night, doing whatever she pleased. "Why not keep it for yourself?" Gaia heard herself asking. It was unusual for her brain to connect to her mouth so directly. "That's what most people would do."

Mary considered this. "I have trouble holding on to it."

Silence enveloped them again.

After a long time Mary turned on her side and propped herself up on her elbow. "So, what are you doing for Thanksgiving dinner?"

Gaia hesitated. She couldn't say she was doing nothing. It was too pathetic. It was begging for sympathy and an invitation. But she couldn't lie, either. She had a feeling Mary wouldn't buy a lie very easily. "Oh. Well. I was thinking I might—"

"Wait a minute," Mary broke in. "Why am I asking? I know what you're doing."

Gaia furrowed her brow. "You do?"

"Yeah."

"Okay. So?"

"You're eating with my family."

"I am?"

"You are. You definitely are."

"Are you sure?"

"Completely, one hundred percent sure."

Gaia couldn't help but let a smile out. "Great. I'll let myself know."

THE DOCTOR TIED THE BELT OF

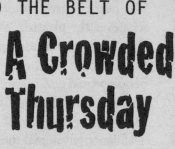

his nondescript and greatly despised tan trench coat. In recent years he'd become attached to very fine clothes. But this coat continued to be useful to him when he was conducting his "side business." It was not only too boring to warrant notice, but of such an inferior material that it was machine washable. That part was important.

Pausing briefly at the corner of Fifty-fifth Street and Fifth Avenue, he studied the information stored in the tracking device. Now, this was a very busy girl. First the West Village, then Astor Place. Then the remote East Village, then West Seventy-seventh Street, Central Park, and what appeared to be a high floor of an apartment building on Central Park West and Sixty-fifth Street. Did teenagers no longer find sleep necessary at all?

He would need to follow her carefully. He wanted this job done by midnight, and her current location— no doubt in a private home—was far less than ideal. That whorish woman—what was her less than amusing alias? Travesura?—had assured him this girl spent a lot of time on the streets and in public places. It had better be so.

He touched his trusted knives, tied up in

felt casing in his roomy pocket. This girl was reported to be quite beautiful and exceptionally strong. That was enticing to him. That's why he'd taken on the job.

"Excuse me!" he snapped, nearly colliding with a shabby-looking woman pushing a stroller containing a shabby-looking infant.

He tried to remember why there were so many people—so many children—milling around the streets of New York City on a Thursday morning at nine o'clock.

For me, Thanksgiving is a mixed bag. On the one hand, there's turkey with stuffing and my grandfather's apple pie. I love that. On the other hand, there are turnips and pumpkin pie. I'd like to know: Who really likes pumpkin pie? Let's all be honest.

On the one hand, there are people like me, hanging out with my grandparents. I love them. On the other hand, there are people like Gaia, who have nobody. That's heartbreaking.

If you think about it, even the first Thanksgiving was in no way a cause for bilateral cheer. I mean, sure, the Native Americans had shown the Pilgrims how to farm the land, and they were psyched about their first harvest. But what did the Native Americans have to celebrate? Alcoholism, VD, and blankets infected with smallpox.

One arm. Two
arms. The fab-
ric settled
with unexpected
ease over her
stomach and
butt, the
skirt grazing
a few inches
above her
knees.

too

nice

"THIS IS TOO NICE." GAIA SAID it out loud to the Victorian-colored glass chandelier that hung over the vast, pillow-laden guest bed in Mary's family's apartment.

The Red Dress

Being friends with Mary was too nice. Mary's unbelievably huge and fantastic apartment on Central Park West was way too nice. The smell of roasting turkey and buttery stuffing was too nice. The thought of spending Thanksgiving with a real family for the first time in five years . . . too nice to think about.

Gaia tried to remind herself to keep her suspicions close around her, but Mary, this place . . . it was dazzling. Can't you just enjoy something? she asked herself impatiently. Accept that some places, some people are purely nice?

She didn't have time to answer herself. There was a knock on the door, and seconds later, Mary opened it partially and poked her head in. "Hi."

"Hi."

"Did you sleep?"

"Like a vegetable."

"Me too. Guess what time it is?"

Gaia shrugged. She wasn't used to having someone talk to her while she was lying in bed. She wasn't a slumber-party kind of girl. She sat up and hugged a pillow on her lap.

"One o'clock. P.M. Big meal is in one hour."

Gaia cleared her throat. What exactly had she'd gotten herself into here? "Is it a dressed-up sort of thing?" Her voice came out squeaky. She didn't want to bring up the fact that she had no home, no possessions, and certainly no Central Park West party clothes at the moment.

Mary had a knack for coming to Gaia's rescue without Gaia even having to ask. "Just a little. I've been laying out stuff in my room. I have the most fabulous dress for you. Come on."

Gaia sat on the edge of the bed. She was wearing a big gray T-shirt she'd worn under her flannel shirt last night. Her legs were bare, her feet covered by white cotton socks. "Like this?" she asked.

"Sure," Mary said. "It's just down the hall. No brothers in sight. I mean, in case you care."

Mary was under the mistaken impression that Gaia was a normal human being who did things like this. The easiest thing would be to play along, to pretend she had comfy pals whose clothes she borrowed, in whose homes she felt perfectly fine wandering around in a T-shirt and socks.

Gaia was a terrible actress. She skulked down the hall and darted into Mary's room like an escapee from Attica.

Once the door was shut, she made herself relax. Mary wasn't kidding about laying out clothes. If there was a carpet in the spacious room, it would have taken an archaeologist to find it. Only the rough shapes of the various pieces of furniture were apparent under thick piles of clothes.

Mary was unapologetic about her colossal slobbiness. Gaia liked that in a person.

"Okay, you ready for the perfect dress?" Mary asked.

Gaia nodded.

"Tra la." Mary held up a tiny, red, crushed velvet dress with a plunging neckline.

Gaia stared. "Are you kidding? I couldn't fit my left foot into that dress."

Mary frowned. "Have you tried it? No. Shut up until you try it."

Gaia held out her hand for it. It weighed about three ounces. "Yes, ma'am. I've never been dressed by a fascist before." Feeling large and self-conscious, Gaia pulled the T-shirt over her head and quickly yanked the dress over her head and shoulders. One arm. Two arms. The fabric settled with unexpected ease over her stomach and butt, the skirt grazing a few inches above her knees.

Mary was surveying the progress with her hands on her hips. When Gaia turned around, her frown blossomed into a smile. "Wow! See?" She took Gaia's hand and pulled her in front of the full-length mirror on the back of her closet.

Gaia gazed at herself in genuine surprise. The dress actually fit. Granted, it was made of stretchy stuff. And it did cling to her gigantic muscles in an unforgiving manner.

"I look like Arnold Schwarzenegger in a dress," Gaia mumbled.

"*What?*" Mary demanded. "I'm going to smack you, girl. You look incredible."

Gaia turned around to examine her backside. "I have incredibly huge muscles."

Mary blew out her breath in frustration. "Guy-aaaaa," she scolded. "You have the body every woman would die to have. You have the long, defined muscles that keep the rest of us slogging it out in overpriced gyms around the country. You have to see that."

"I see Mr. Universe."

"Shut *up!*" Mary roared. Now she was mad. She held out her hand. "So give it back. Seriously. I mean it. If you can't appreciate that it looks beautiful, you don't deserve to borrow my goddamned dress."

Gaia cast her a pleading gaze. "Look, I'm trying. I really am." She studied herself in the mirror for another minute, trying to see herself through other eyes.

The dress really was extraordinary. Gaia loved the too long sleeves and the way they flared at the wrist. "Please let me borrow it?" Gaia asked, weirded out by hearing those words in her voice. "I'll say anything, true or untrue. I am Kate Moss. I am a waif. I can't do a single push-up."

Mary laughed. "Fine. It's yours. In fact, you can have it for keeps. After seeing you in it, I won't be able to stand the sight of me."

Now it was Gaia's turn to glare. "Hang on. *You're* allowed the exaggeratedly negative body image, but not me? Who made these rules?"

Mary waved a hand in the air. "Point taken. Never mind. But keep the stupid dress." She gestured at the snowstorm of clothes. "I have others, as you may have noticed." She rooted around the bottom of her closet and threw Gaia a pair of black cotton tights.

"Thanks," Gaia said.

"Oh, and here."

"Ouch." A dark red, forties-style pump flew out of the closet and hit Gaia on the shin. Thankfully, she dodged its mate.

"Sorry," Mary murmured. Now she was gathering jewelry for Gaia.

"What size are your feet?" Gaia asked, staring suspiciously at the shoe.

"Eight."

"I wear eight and a half," Gaia said.

Mary was busy untangling a clump of necklaces. "So? Close enough."

Apparently Mary didn't get hung up on little matters like housing all five toes.

Again, though, Mary was right. The shoe was close enough to fitting. Gaia put on the second one and stomped around the room, trying to get used to the heels.

Mary spent the next twenty minutes coaxing Gaia into the makeup chair, and the twenty minutes after that brushing Gaia's hair, spangling her with jewelry, and hunting down the exact right shade of lip gloss. At last she was done. "Oh my God, my brothers are going to be drooling," she announced, nodding at her finished work.

Gaia did feel prettier, but she also felt like someone else.

"Are you ready to meet the clan?"

If Gaia had the potential to feel nervous, now would have been an obvious time. "I guess so." She looked at Mary. Mary was still wearing blue nylon warm-up pants and a wife-beater tank top. Light freckles stood out on her thin shoulders and arms. Her hair was possibly the craziest mess Gaia had ever seen.

"Oh, I'm fine," Mary claimed. Her eyes darted around the room, and she picked up the first thing in her path, a blue chenille sweater, and stuck her head through. "All set," she confirmed.

Gaia was speechless as she followed Mary out of

the room. She remembered what Mary had said about not holding on to love very well.

"HOW ARE THE POTATOES COMING, Sam?" Mrs. Gannis's voice floated into the kitchen.

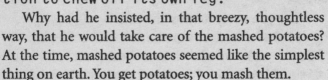

Sam looked up from the huge aluminum pot. He felt like a wolf with its leg caught in a trap. He finally understood the wolf's perverse temptation to chew off its own leg.

Why had he insisted, in that breezy, thoughtless way, that he would take care of the mashed potatoes? At the time, mashed potatoes seemed like the simplest thing on earth. You get potatoes; you mash them.

Besides, he'd figured this important job in the kitchen would keep him out of the fray of tense Gannis-family relations. It would give him a little breathing room from Heather, too, which they both needed. It had gotten to the point where every single thing brought them right back into the danger zone. A casual question from Heather's mother about what they'd done the previous night, an innocent reference to chess, a song on the radio about a girl with blond hair. Not being in the same room with Heather or talking about anything at all seemed the safest bet.

But Sam now understood that making mashed potatoes belonged in a category with particle physics, only harder. Before you mashed them, you had to cook them to make them soft, it turned out. How were you supposed to do that? First he'd thrown the whole pile in the oven, but what was the right temperature, and how long would it take? Then he took a cue from the one meal he'd ever made successfully—spaghetti. You made hard noodles soft by boiling them. So he boiled up the potatoes. It seemed to take hours before they were soft.

Now he was beating the crap out of those poor, boiled potatoes, working up a sweat. On the table was a whole tool kit of discarded instruments. The dinner fork was too small, obviously. The plastic whisk was wimpy. The metal slotted spoon made a tremendous racket. At last Mr. Gannis had acquainted him with a tool called a masher. A masher! A holiday miracle. Who could have guessed there'd be an implement built for this exact purpose?

Now he was madly mashing. Only the potatoes still didn't look right. Mashed potatoes were supposed to be smooth and pale yellow in color. These were lumpy and riddled with brown skin. Oh. Something occurred to him. You were supposed to take the skin off first, weren't you? He tried to fish out the bigger pieces of skin. It was hopeless.

Well, maybe they tasted good. He took a taste.

They tasted slightly more flavorful than air. All right, well, that's what salt was for. He shook in a small blizzard of salt.

He cast an eye at the fridge. Hmmm. He took out a box of butter. He remembered his mom once saying that her motto for cooking was, When in doubt, add butter. He threw in a stick. He threw in another stick. He was still in doubt. He threw in a third.

He stirred, hoping his mother hadn't just been being witty.

"SO, GAIA, HOW LONG HAVE YOU lived in New York?"

Disappointment

Now Gaia remembered the problem with meeting strangers, particularly the parents-of-friends variety of strangers. They asked you things.

Gaia chewed a piece of turkey breast and tried to look agreeably at Mary's mother. She swallowed it with effort. "Well, I guess I—"

"No questions," Mary interrupted, coming to Gaia's rescue yet again. "No interrogating Mary's new friend, Mom."

Mary's mom laughed, which Gaia thought was pretty sporting of her. She gave Gaia a conspiratorial look. "My daughter is very bossy. You may have noticed this."

Gaia liked Mary's mom so far. She had dark red hair, sort of like Mary's but far better behaved. She wore cropped black wool pants and a bright orange velvet button-down shirt that clashed mightily with her hair. It wasn't standard middle-aged mom apparel, but it wasn't a grown-up person trying too hard to be cool, either.

The family's cook, Olga, appeared at Gaia's elbow with a steaming silver serving dish of baby vegetables. They were tidy and beautiful, not the creamed vegetable slop that usually showed up on Thanksgiving. Gaia guessed from Olga's accent that she was Russian and that she hadn't been speaking English for long. "Thank you," she murmured, trying to serve herself without bouncing baby potatoes into her lap. Or Mary's dress's lap.

"The food's fantastic," Mary's brother said to Olga.

Was he Paul or Brendan? Gaia couldn't remember. He was the cuter one, though, with light blue eyes and a quarter-inch of stubble on his chin.

"Absolutely," Mary's father agreed. He raised his glass for at least the fourth time in the meal. "Let's give thanks for Olga, a godsend." They all clinked glasses and agreed yet again. Gaia noted that there was sparkling water in his glass and not wine.

Olga seemed pleased with the attention. "Stop eet, Meester Moss," she ordered coyly.

Out of the corner of her eye, Gaia saw Mary stand up.

"I gotta pee. I'll be back in a minute," Mary announced to the table at large.

Mary's mom smiled in her forbearing way, and Gaia saw an emotion she wasn't sure how to analyze. There was something in the woman's face that struck Gaia as both worried and apologetic at the same time.

Suddenly Olga was back at Gaia's elbow, this time holding a basket of corn bread. It smelled like happiness. "Would you like some?" Olga asked.

Remotely, without really thinking about it, Gaia registered that Olga's words came out clear and crisp, without an accent.

"Of course. It smells delicious. Did you make this, too?" Gaia asked politely.

She served herself a fat piece of corn bread, and when she looked up, the entire Moss family, minus Mary, was staring at her. Olga was staring, too.

Gaia glanced from face to face. Oh, shit. What had she done now? These stares were too extreme to signify she'd used the wrong fork. She felt her mouth to see if she was wearing a mustache of cranberry sauce or anything.

"You speak Russian," Mr. Moss declared.

"I do?" Gaia found herself asking dumbly. She looked back at Olga and realized what must have happened. Olga must have murmured to her in Russian, and she must have answered in Russian without thinking. "I—I guess I do. Some, anyway," Gaia said, her fingers pinching and pulling at the napkin under the table.

Gaia felt badly thrown by this. Her mother spoke Russian to her from the time she was a baby, and Gaia grew accustomed to switching back and forth between languages hundreds of times a day. But those words gave her a feeling on her tongue that she associated purely with her mother. She hadn't spoken Russian in five years.

The table was still silent. Gaia felt her vision blurring. She stood up, keeping her gaze down. "Excuse me for just a moment," she mumbled.

"Of course," Mrs. Moss said.

Gaia walked blindly from the dining room and down the hallway. She hadn't meant to go to Mary's room, exactly. She just wasn't thinking.

The moment she opened the door to Mary's room, Mary froze. Gaia took two steps forward and froze, too.

Mary was bent far over her dressing table. Her eyes, turned now to Gaia, were large. In her hand was a rolled-up tube of paper. On the tabletop was a mirror, and on the mirror were several skinny rows of white powder cut from a tiny white hill. A razor blade winked at her in the light.

Gaia was naive and inexperienced, but she wasn't stupid. She knew what Mary was doing, and it made her feel sick.

She stared at Mary for another moment before she turned and left the room. She strode to the guest room and gathered her bag and coat.

She forced herself to take a detour on the way to the elevator.

"Mr. and Mrs. Moss," she announced from the entrance to the dining room. "I'm so sorry, but I have to go. Thank you very sincerely for letting me come."

She made her way to the elevator vestibule without a backward glance. She shrugged on her coat as the car descended. Yellow-green jacket. Red dress. She thought of Ed.

Outside on the street a siren blared, surprising her with its jarring unpleasantness.

"MY GOD, SAM, THESE ARE THE best potatoes I've ever eaten," Mr. Gannis said heartily, serving up his fourth helping. Sam hoped he wasn't going to be responsible for putting the man in the hospital with a heart attack.

Butter

He looked at the other plates around the table.

Each of the four underfed Gannis women still had on her plate an untouched pile of potatoes so calorie packed, they were bleeding butter. Heather met his eyes apologetically. "They're awfully, um . . . rich."

Dear Ed,

I'm sorry not to be saying this to you in person, but good-bye. I have to leave New York for a while. Things got out of hand with Ella, and, well . . . hopefully I'll get the chance to tell you about it someday.

It's time for me to set up a new life. I'm almost of legal age to be on my own now. And with all of my useful skills and abilities—not to mention my sunny temperament—I should have all kinds of great job possibilities:

> *Waitress*
> *Counter-person at 7-Eleven*
> *Tollbooth attendant*
> *Dishwasher*

So before I go, I just wanted to tell you this one thing, and I hope you'll forgive me for being sappy. But as I wracked my brains to think of stuff to be thankful for, the only thing I felt sure of is you. You are a much better friend than I've ever deserved.

I will never ever forget you for as long (or short) as I live.

Gaia

He wheeled back
and opened the
door just wide
enough so that

pennsylvania

he could **station**
toss the
bloody scalpel
into the trash
can.

GAIA LOOKED UP AT THE BIG
destination board that hung
above the expansive waiting area
of Penn Station. The board oper-
ated like the tote board on

One Way

Family Feud—its tiles turning to reveal all the destina-
tions. "Survey says . . . Trenton—Northeast Corridor—
track 12—5:09." "Survey says . . . Boston—New
England Express—track 9—5:42."

The place was ugly and crowded, and it smelled
bad. And by the way, she wondered sourly, whose bril-
liant idea was it to call the train station smack-dab in
the middle of New York City Pennsylvania Station?
Hello? Ever take a geography class?

She felt tired and sad and cranky, no longer riding
the powerful surge of anger and indignation that
made it much more satisfying to run away.

She eyed the different cities, having absolutely no
idea where she wanted to go. If she could go anywhere,
she'd choose Paris. The Latin Quarter. She'd sit at the
terrace of a quaint café across from the Notre Dame
cathedral. Sip a double espresso as she read some
poems from Baudelaire's *Fleurs du mal*. But that wasn't
going to happen. Not today, anyway. She didn't have a
passport, let alone money for the flight.

Hmmm. Maybe Chicago. She'd always wanted to
visit the museum there. If she couldn't go to Paris, she
could at least sit for an hour in front of Gustave

110

Caillebotte's wall-sized painting, *Paris Street, Rainy Day*. She first saw it in an art magazine she was flipping through while waiting to have a wisdom tooth pulled. The dreary scene spoke to her. Ambling along a cobblestone street on a gray, rainy day. That was her.

Engine, engine, number 9, going down the Chicago line. If the train falls off the track, do you want your money back? Yes. Y-e-s spells yes, you dirty, dirty dishrag—you.

She waited in the Amtrak ticket line behind a twenty-something couple from Jersey who—Gaia gathered from overhearing—had met the night before in an East Village club. They couldn't keep their hands off each other. Pinching, groping, giggling. It took everything Gaia had not to gag before she finally reached the window, where she came face-to-face with Ned, the ticket vendor.

She leaned forward to speak into the round voice amplifier.

"Chicago. One way."

He visibly perked up at the sight of her. His eyes leered at her from behind the thick Plexiglas.

"Going all by yourself?"

"Yeah. Is that a problem?"

"No . . . I just thought . . ." He raised his eyebrows suggestively.

"Thought what?"

"I don't know, a girl as pretty as yourself. Just seems like you'd have a . . . companion."

She sighed. "Well, I'm alone. Is there a sleeping car on that train going to Chicago?"

He swiveled on his seat and clacked a succession of keys at his computer. "Not until nine-thirty tonight."

"How about another train, then? Is there any train with a sleeping car leaving soon? Doesn't matter where it's going."

He looked at her. Then back at his screen. Ten more seconds of clacking. "There's a train to Orlando leaving in about an hour."

Gaia took a moment to ponder Orlando. It was a light-year away from this rainy day. It was an artificial city populated by tourists and the people who served the tourists. It was the land of water slides and theme parks, of Mickey Mouse and Jaws: The Ride.

"There's definitely a sleeper car?" Gaia wanted to confirm.

"There is a sleeping compartment, yes," Ned replied.

"I'll take it."

What the hell. She needed a vacation. And a little sun never hurt anybody. If it was warm enough, maybe she'd even buy a bikini. Hit the beach.

But she still had a whole hour to kill. After Ned slid her ticket under the window, she leaned a final time into the voice amplifier.

"Is there someplace that sells stamps around here?"

THE DOCTOR QUICKENED HIS STEPS

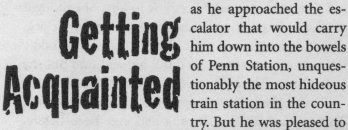

Getting Acquainted

as he approached the escalator that would carry him down into the bowels of Penn Station, unquestionably the most hideous train station in the country. But he was pleased to be here. He was downright overjoyed that his target had abandoned her safe perch up on Central Park West and come down here.

The ugly, subterranean corridors of this station were hardly fit for any human pursuit, but the place fit his needs quite perfectly.

According to his device, she was less than two hundred feet away. He began scanning the crowds in the hope of identifying her, acquainting himself a little with her face before he went to work.

GAIA REREAD HER LETTER TO Ed.

Out of Order

She was seated at the counter of a small coffee-and-muffin place in the train station's row of shops and eateries. What a stupid letter.

She went to crumple the letter, then stopped herself. She needed to say something to him. She thought of him calling her on Friday night at eleven o'clock, expecting another of their ricocheting, sleepy, oddly intimate conversations. He'd call her and find out she wasn't there. `Really, really wasn't there.`

Gaia sighed. She propped her chin in her hand. This was harder than leaving had ever been before. None of the other places had Ed.

Or Sam.

She folded her letter carefully and put it in the envelope. She wrote out Ed's address and placed the stamp in the corner so it wasn't crooked.

She felt the eyes of a man slumped at the next table over, hovering on her legs. She turned to him.

"Letter to Mom and Dad, sweetheart?" he asked. The smell of stale alcohol on his breath made Gaia wince.

Okay, she thought. That's it. She was sick of being leered at. Time to lose the dress. First the smarmy ticket vendor, now this loser.

"That's right. *Honey*," she said. Turning her attention back to the envelope, she licked the inside edge of the flap and sealed it.

"I like to watch you do that."

`Gaia narrowed her eyes at the old pervert.` Blech. As she got up, she knocked over her half-filled paper cup of coffee so that it spilled into the man's lap.

"Oh, I'm sorry," she lied. Then she swung her bag over her shoulder and took off.

A minute later she arrived at the women's rest room. A hand-scrawled sign taped to the door read Out of Order.

Perfect. She didn't need to pee. She could change her clothes in peace. But pushing open the door, she was immediately struck by the most powerful stench this side of the Hudson. She wanted to bolt, get out of there, but the room was empty—it would take her only a minute. Slip off the dress; pull on the jeans and sweatshirt. Off. On. Go. Like a pit stop at the Indy 500.

Just as long as no one lit a match.

She hurried to a stall. Holding her breath, she quickly slipped off Mary's shoes. She was peeling off the tights when all of a sudden she heard the door fly open.

"Let go of me!" a young female voice demanded.

Gaia looked through the crack of her stall: Two thugs had just entered, dragging behind them a teenage girl, dressed in a Nike sports bra, a leopard-print skirt, and just one stiletto heel. The other one must've been out there somewhere, floating among the sea of arrivals and departures. Quickly Gaia pulled the tights back up over her waist.

"Let's have it, bitch," ordered the shorter of the two, the one with the New Jersey Devils baseball cap.

"I don't got it. I swear," the girl cried.

The girl's hair was blond and tangled. She looked no older than Gaia—maybe sixteen or seventeen. Like Gaia, she'd probably done the rounds in foster care. Like Gaia, she'd probably run away at least once. Gaia suspected she was a prostitute and that the bigger guy was her pimp.

Each of the men grabbed one of the girl's pale arms, and together they shoved her into the dirty, white-tiled wall. She cried out in pain but managed to protect her head.

Gaia watched from the stall, letting her anger grow inside her chest. She hadn't had any real release in days. The anger was right there, so easy to call upon. There was her rage at Ella. Her fury at crazy, misguided Mary who had everything in the world and chose to screw it up.

"We're not playing games this time, sunshine," said the big, bearlike thug, whose belly hung out from a black T-shirt that asked, Got Milk?

Gaia saw his big, paw hands fumbling, then heard a noise. Flick. The Bear underlined his threat by holding up a fierce-looking switchblade that gleamed under the fluorescent light. "Now, let's see it, or you'll have a brand-new face to look at in the mirror." He held the knife against her cheek.

Gaia threw open the door of her stall.

The two men turned to stare at her.

Gaia forgot until she read the particular looks in their eyes that she was still wearing Mary's clingy, short red dress.

"Check you out," the man in the Devils hat said, studying her appreciatively. "We've got a regular party happening in here."

"Get off her," Gaia said.

"Pardon?" the big one asked, curiosity and amusement flashing in his eyes.

Gaia came closer. She spoke loudly and enunciated her words clearly. "Get off the girl. Let her go."

The Bear shook his head. "Is this your business? I don't think so. Why don't you stand aside, sweetheart? It'll be your turn next."

Gaia liked to protect her conscience by being absolutely clear about her intentions before she did harm. "I'm warning you. I'll kick your ass if you don't lay off her."

They both guffawed at her. "Len, grab her," the big one instructed the smaller guy. "This is gonna be fun."

Len did as he was told. When he reached for Gaia's arm, she backhanded him hard against the side of his neck. She caught him by surprise. He staggered sideways. Gaia kicked him hard in the chest and watched him slam into the hand-drying machine and slide to the floor. Len was disappointingly easy.

"Holy shit."

Gaia turned her head to see the Bear staring at her

with astonishment. She'd talked enough. She went after him.

The Bear was holding that blade, which made her approach trickier. She didn't hesitate, though. He stood to confront her, as she gambled he would, and she grabbed the knife-wielding arm by the wrist and bent it sharply behind him. She wrenched the other arm back to join the first and pulled him down so she could lodge her knee in his back.

The Bear groaned in pain. The blade clattered to the ground. The girl backed off into the corner, shivering.

Gaia let his arms go. Now that the blade was out of the way, she could give him some room.

He literally growled as he turned on her. He raised his arm to punch her in the jaw, but she caught it long before it landed and took the force of his own sloppy effort to flip him onto the linoleum. It was kind of a trademark move of hers. Effortless. Fairly graceful. Totally satisfying.

She backed up a few steps and let him get up. She hated herself for enjoying it, but she did. The Bear deserved anything she gave him and much more. He'd obviously spent too long believing that women could be intimidated. Let him remember this.

It was all he could do to get himself back on his feet. He staggered toward Gaia, swinging at her. His lack of skill was pitiful. There wasn't much point in trying to make it a real contest. She clipped his jaw with her right fist. She very likely broke his nose with her left. She wanted to leave him a memento.

His eyes displayed real fear now. Although Gaia couldn't feel fear, she was astute at recognizing its signs. Wild, darting eyes, rapid, shallow breaths. Gaia took that as her cue to finish him. She landed a hard, fast blow to a calculated spot under his ear. As expected, he crumpled to the floor, unconscious. Gaia knew he'd feel like shit when he came to. But he *would* come to and not much worse for the wear, either.

Suddenly the girl was shrieking. Gaia heard movement behind her. Much closer than she was expecting. Before she could regroup, the smaller guy appeared in the corner of her eye and shoved her hard in the back, sending her sprawling across the floor. Gaia got up fast, but he was barreling toward her.

Gaia turned, smashing his face with a roundhouse kick so powerful, she was sure she'd knocked him out. But she rushed the kick and threw herself badly off balance. She lost her footing, and her head came down hard against the corner of the porcelain sink.

Gaia groaned, holding the side of her head. She put both of her hands on the side of the sink for support and swayed back up to her feet.

At last the wretched-smelling room was quiet. The girl was backed against the tiled wall, gazing at Gaia with a stunned expression. "Are you okay?"

Gaia nodded. "I think so."

The girl put her hands up to her cheeks. "God, I

don't know what to say. Thank you. I never had anyone stick up for me before. Is there anything I can do for you? Buy you a coffee?

Gaia shook her head, then leaned herself up against the wall for support. Her eyes closed. Her head was pounding ferociously. She'd hit it hard.

"Hey," the girl said, reaching out to her.

"I'll be fine," Gaia tried to assure her. "Just give me a minute." She shielded her eyes with her hand. Her pupils were reacting sluggishly to the bright, fluorescent light above.

Gaia started to slide down along the wall until she ended sitting up on the floor. Right next to the girl.

"I'm gonna call 911."

"No!" Gaia ordered. "I just need to rest." She started to drift, to give in. "Rest," she murmured again. And then she blacked out.

"ALL ABOARD FOR THE SOUTHERN Star, now boarding on track 12. All aboard!"

A large segment of the Penn Station crowd shuffled in unison toward the steps that led down to the waiting train.

Unholy Moment

He shuffled right along with them, `his yellow-green eyes darting wildly.` Searching for his target. His tracking device told him he was at point-blank range.

He reached the platform and caught a glimpse of her—a blond in a yellow-green Polartec jacket, carrying a black messenger bag. She was just stepping into one of the train's sleeper cars. He calmly made his way through the frantic human herd and boarded the same car, but at the other end. He walked with haste and purpose through the car, noticing the blond up ahead. She was scanning the compartment numbers as she advanced, finally entering one near the middle—on his left. Number 33A.

He arrived there not more than ten seconds later, pausing a moment to close his trench coat over his tie—`a Salvatore Ferragamo yellow silk, dotted with little teddy bears.` A client had given it to him a few years back to thank him for the perfect cheekbones he had given her. And they were perfect. He had truly outdone himself. So in the name of mastery and precision, he always wore the tie for these unholy moments. It had become part of the ceremony. Priests wear their robes; he wore his Ferragamo teddy bear tie under his cheap, washable trench coat.

He slowly, silently turned the brass handle of the compartment door and entered.

"Hey!" the blond snarled. "This one's taken."

"Is that right?" he replied with `zero inflection` in his voice. Then he grinned like a used car salesman as he stepped inside.

"Hey!" she repeated. "What do you think you're doing?"

He just kept smiling and closed the door behind him, pulling down the shade to cover the small window.

FIVE MINUTES LATER, HE STEPPED

off the train. One of the conductors, doing some final work on the platform, gave him a curious look.

"Wrong train." The doctor tossed him a shrug, pretending to be embarrassed. "I must be blind."

He made his way back up the steps, back to the vast waiting room with the giant destination board. On the way he couldn't help thinking that the redheaded woman was a little off in her assessment. The girl was hardly "tough." Annoying, maybe, but tough? And her face wasn't so pretty, either. He imagined a little sculpting work on that nose would make for a significant improvement. . . . Perhaps a little Gore-Tex in those thin lips. An injection for those premature lines in her forehead. Under different circumstances he would have certainly left his card.

Oh, well . . .

He stopped at the rest room, whose door had a crude Out of Order sign taped to it. A perfect place to get rid of the instrument. But when he opened the door, the stench that hit him was so overwhelming, he had to quickly close it. He started off, then changed his mind. He wheeled back and opened the door just wide enough so that he could toss the bloody scalpel into the trash can.

A few feet to the left of the trash can he saw the prostrate body of a teenage girl. She was graceful, blond, quite pretty, in fact. Probably strung out on drugs. From the bruise on her face it looked like somebody had beaten her up. Her pimp, no doubt. It was pitiful, really.

He tossed the scalpel and watched it sink cleanly to the bottom of the trash can.

Too bad, he thought as he was making his exit. It had been such a trusty tool. Why, he had used it just that morning on Mrs. Gardner. Carved her the best-looking chin money could buy.

After I hit my head in the train station, I saw red and green sparklers bursting in front of my eyes. I must have passed out after that because I had this weird, dreamlike reverie about Ed and his being color-blind. Don't ask me why.

In my dream I was color-blind, too. I couldn't see green, which my whacked-out mind was convinced was the color of fear. Green looked the same as red, but red wasn't the color of fear, according to my dream self. What was red the color of?

It became this desperate, urgent thing I needed to figure out. What was red the color of? Green was fear; what was red?

What was red?

Well, red is the color of tomatoes, you might say sensibly, and shut up already. But you know how dreams are.

Anyway, I guess it was around then that I came to.

Heather was too hurt to feel it. Her heart was on autopilot once more. "You've fallen for **not a penny** her, haven't you?"

HER VISION AND AWARENESS CAME

back slowly. She blinked open her eyes and then closed them again. Then came the smell.

A Freaking Mess

What the hell was that? Where was she?

Gaia forced open her eyes. Oh God. The bathroom. The awful bathroom in the train station.

She sat up and looked around her. The thugs she'd fought were still passed out on the other side of the room. One of them was breathing loudly, fitfully. The other was clutching his jaw and moaning. They'd be up and at it soon enough.

And the girl. Where had the girl gone? Suddenly Gaia froze. She clambered to her feet, ignoring the searing pain in her temple. She checked the floor around her. She checked the stall where she'd begun to change. Mary's shoes were just where she'd kicked them off, but her bag was gone. Her bag with her wallet and her money and her clothes and shoes. Oh Christ, and where was her coat? Her coat with the train ticket to Orlando inside the pocket.

It was gone. All of it. Shit.

Well, that was gratitude for you. Save somebody's ass, and they'll rob you blind. Give a lot, and they'll take a lot more.

Shit!

She moved to the sink, splashed cold water on her badly bruised face. When she looked in the mirror, she got a shock. The left side of her face, her cheekbone all the way up to her temple, was already covered by an ugly purple bruise. The corner of her lip was bleeding, not to mention her mascara. Mary's velvet dress was ripped in two places. She was a freaking mess.

She retrieved the shoes and squeezed them on her sore feet, trying not to let herself cry. Now what? She'd arrived at the station full of cash and ready to start a new life.

She'd be leaving it broke and broken.

Hunted Prey

"WHERE IS GAIA? I THOUGHT SHE'D be joining us."

Ella took a protracted sip of her third glass of merlot, letting the velvety nectar wash over her tongue. Then she made a whole show of sliding back the sleeve of her blouse to glance at her watch.

"Oh, my, it is getting late, isn't it?" she said, wondering just how Gaia was doing. Although the obnoxious girl had run, she had certainly not gotten away. It was helpful that Gaia had taken off *after* Ella had slipped the tracking device into her coat pocket.

Ella sat with two of George's old agency friends and their wives. They were gathered at a table for six in the opulent dining room of La Bijou, an haute-cuisine restaurant on West Sixty-fourth Street, off Broadway. Most of the patrons here were silver-haired, silver-spooned socialites who just an hour earlier had been watching the new opera across the street at Lincoln Center. The waiters were French to a fault.

And then there was the menu. A menagerie of hunted prey, ranging from roasted duck to wild Scottish hare to rock Cornish hen with the word of caution to be careful of possible bird shot.

This was George's consolation prize to Ella for his being called away on Thanksgiving. The restaurant was fine with her; the company, a bore.

"I would so like to see Gaia, that poor thing," Mrs. Bessemer agreed. "Her parents were such lovely people."

Ella stifled a yawn. She shrugged daintily. "Gaia is a teenager, as you know. Her appearances are difficult to predict. I told her of course how much you'd all like to see her, but . . . Gaia has a mind and a schedule of her own." Ella lied effortlessly, without even needing to listen to herself.

Besides, she has an appointment with a doctor, Ella added silently. She tapped her menu. "Listen, why don't we just go ahead and order? I'll order a little something extra for Gaia so when—if—she comes, she can join right in. I'm sure she won't mind."

That said, her beeper went off. She opened her purse, extracted the beeper, and looked at the number. "That's probably her now. If you'll excuse me, I'll be back in a moment."

THE DOCTOR STOOD INSIDE THE

Insult and Injury

phone booth just outside Penn Station's southwest entrance, annoyed at this particular aspect of his written instructions. Who used a phone booth anymore? It was rather galling. He'd punched in the beeper number as instructed, and now he waited for the ring. There it was.

'Mrs. Travesura, I presume?"

"Yes, Doctor. Is it done?"

"Of course."

"Excellent. And in what condition is our patient?"

The woman could barely contain the pleasure in her voice.

"Alive, as promised," the doctor responded. "Though not likely to recount her experiences anytime soon." He wouldn't reward her with the graphic details.

"No one saw you?"

The doctor sighed impatiently. "Absolutely not."

"I'm sure. Now, did you remove the bug from the pocket of her coat?"

This had grown annoying, verging on insulting. "Mrs. Travesura. I am a professional. You need not grill me on these absurd details."

"I apologize . . . *Doctor.* If you'll permit me one last question?"

He sighed again. "Yes."

"Are you holding the tracking device in your hand?"

"I am."

"Good. Good-bye, then, you disgusting, evil bastard."

The doctor was blinking in fury, barely able to process the childish affront, when the device began beeping in his hand. He held the readout close to his face, trying to discern the message in the darkness of the booth.

He could make out numbers scrolling across the screen. 5 . . . 4 . . . 3 . . . 2 . . . 1 . . .

The explosion ripped the tiny booth apart.

GAIA TURNED AT THE SOUND OF

No Refunds

the explosion. Virtually everyone in the station jumped at the noise. Within a minute she heard a symphony of sirens.

She glanced ahead of her in frustration at the single open ticket booth. She glanced behind her at the ten or so people who continued the line, all of whom looked as cranky as she felt. She didn't care if her own feet exploded. There was no way she was losing her place in this line.

Scores of policemen were zipping in and out the south doors of the station. Many civilians were running around, too, wanting a piece of the action.

"There was a bomb!" she heard somebody shouting. "Right out front. Blew up a phone booth!"

There were lots of oohs and ahs and murmurs throughout the station, but Gaia was morbidly amused to see that not a single person left her line.

Just wait until the camera crews from the local news get here—then it will really be a circus, Gaia found herself thinking.

Another ticket salesperson opened a second window. That would speed things up. Minutes later, Gaia was waved forward. Before she reached the window, she realized she was being reunited with her old friend Ned.

"How can I help you?" His eyes showed not a flicker of recognition. Apparently she was a lot less attractive battered and bruised.

"Remember me? I bought a ticket to Orlando from you about an hour and a half ago. The sleeper car?"

His face was blank.

"Well, listen, my ticket got stolen. I need to get a refund."

Ned shrugged. "Sorry. Train 404 to Orlando is long gone. Unless you can produce the ticket, I can't give you a refund."

Gaia rolled her eyes. "How can I produce a ticket if it got stolen?"

Ned's face was devoid of interest or sympathy. "No ticket, no refund."

Gaia was starting to feel desperate. If she couldn't get a refund, she'd have no money. Not a cent. Nothing. How long could she last on the streets of New York flat broke? Even the flophouses cost a few dollars. "Ned, please. We're . . . *friends*, practically. Can't you help me out here? I really, really need the cash."

Ned shook his head. He wouldn't look anywhere near her eyes. A pretty, confident, sexily clad girl with a wallet full of cash was interesting to Ned. A bruised, desperate, penniless girl was not. He focused his gaze over her head. "Next?" he called to the person at the front of the line.

Suddenly Gaia felt overcome by a wave of dizziness so powerful, it almost made her sick to her stomach. She grabbed the edge of the high counter to steady herself. "Ned! Ned. Please. Don't be an asshole. Just listen to me for a minute, okay?" Gaia could hear her voice rising in her ears. "Ned! *Ned!*" God, if he weren't enclosed in the bullet-proof booth, she'd love to belt him. "Ned!"

The next thing Gaia knew, there was a police officer, a young Hispanic man with a crew cut, grabbing her by the arm. "Come on, miss," he said. "There's a long line here, okay? Gotta keep it moving."

"But I—" Gaia grabbed her arm back. "My ticket got stolen. And all my money. And I really need—"

Gaia stopped. He wasn't listening. It was hopeless. She could tell the policeman was looking her over, and she could tell exactly what he was thinking, too. Gaia was wearing a shredded, clingy minidress, high heels, and a big bruise on her head.

"Come on, miss," he said again. His voice was patient, tired, pitying. "Do you want to step out of the way, or do you want me to arrest you? I'd think a girl like you would have good reason to stay out of the way if you can help it."

A girl like you. It was obvious he thought she was a hooker. A hooker addicted to drugs who'd just been shaken up by her pimp. It was ironic, but that was exactly what she looked like. While the *actual* drug-addicted hooker who'd been shaken up by her pimp was zipping off to Orlando in a pair of jeans and a fluorescent yellow-green Polartec jacket, carrying almost 450 bucks in her pockets.

Gaia wondered if her luck could be any worse.

HEATHER LAY BACK ON THE COUCH

The (Other) Magic Word

and rested her head on Sam's lap as he flipped channels with the remote control. Without looking at her, he rested his hand on her stomach. She felt her iridescent pink silk blouse riding up over her belly button. She studied his face above her. It was so unbelievably handsome. His strong jaw was smooth and clean shaven for this event. His brownish gold hair had gotten long and was curling around the collar of his cobalt blue oxford shirt. His complicated hazel eyes were framed by long black lashes. She wanted those eyes on her. On her face, her hair, her breasts, the bare swath of skin above her skirt.

But at the moment his eyes were riveted on the television screen as he burned through almost a hundred channels' worth of programming. It was hopeless sitting in a room with a boy, a television, and a remote control. You never got any attention or even the pleasure of watching any one show for longer than three minutes.

She smiled up at him. She didn't mind. This was the kind of relationship problem she enjoyed having.

She heard clinking sounds from the kitchen. Her parents cleaning up the last of the dishes. She heard the faint sound of laughter—Lauren talking on the phone. From her and Phoebe's room she heard the inevitable hum of the stair-climbing machine, Phoebe's most prized possession. God forbid an ounce of turkey should stick to her hips.

"Having a nice Thanksgiving?" she asked Sam.

"Hmmm," he said, his eyes not flickering from the screen.

"My dad loved your potatoes."

"Mmmm."

Sam wasn't going to talk, obviously. But he did move the remote control to the hand that rested on her stomach. He used his free hand to caress her forehead, softly pushing her hair back from her face. She breathed in deeply and let out a sigh of pleasure. It felt so nice, she wished they could just stay like that forever.

For the first time in weeks she felt truly relaxed. The dinner had gone fairly well. No hysterics or anything.

She was relieved to have finally confronted Sam with the Gaia issue and gotten the answer she wanted.

"Hey, wait, hold it there a minute," she ordered. The local news was showing footage of the Thanksgiving parade. She used to love that when she was a kid. The camera zoomed in on one enormous balloon after another: Barney, some pig or other, a Rugrat, two gigantic M&M's. She remembered sitting on her dad's shoulders for hours—so long that both her feet would fall asleep—and watching the floats and marching bands go by.

The report on the parade ended abruptly, and the picture changed to show a gloomy-looking Penn Station lit up by dozens of red flashing lights.

"God, what happened there?" Heather mumbled.

"Shhh," Sam ordered, leaning in to listen.

". . . Two mysterious tragedies here in one evening," the telegenic special reporter was saying into the camera. "Are they related, and if so, how? That is what detectives are asking tonight as they start a two-pronged investigation here in Penn Station."

The camera moved to show a phone booth that had been blown to bits. Twisted metal and glass were everywhere. "A bomb was detonated here, outside of New York City's busy Penn Station, less than an hour ago. . . . One person dead, not yet identified . . ."

The camera moved to show a stretcher carrying a

girl. ". . . And in a second calamity, a young girl, not yet identified, was brutally slashed and disfigured in her sleeping compartment in a train pulling out of Penn Station at 6:47 P.M. She remains in a coma at Roosevelt Hospital . . ."

Beneath her, Heather felt Sam's legs go rigid. "Oh my God," he whispered. "Jesus."

Suddenly Sam was on his feet, dumping Heather's head rudely onto the couch. She sat herself upright quickly. "Sam, what's your problem?"

Sam was stammering, pointing at the TV. "Th-That's—could that be? I think that might be Gaia's coat! That green coat? Oh my God."

Sam was pacing, holding his head, unable to watch the screen and then watching it again. "Her hair. Do you see her hair? It's blond. Is that Gaia? Could that be her?"

Heather glared at him in disbelief. He was *freaking*. Absolutely freaking. She'd never seen him anything like this. She wanted to slap him.

She went closer to the TV and studied the picture. Yes, she recognized that hideous jacket. She squinted and tried to get a look at the face, a crazy mixture of emotions swarming around her heart.

Just before the camera switched back to a shot of the shattered phone booth, Heather caught a glimpse of the girl's face. It was heavily bandaged, but she could see enough to know it wasn't Gaia.

Sam paced. His face was the color of skim milk.

Heather angrily snatched the remote control from his hand and used it to switch off the TV.

"What are you doing?" Sam demanded fiercely. He tried to take the remote back. His eyes were wild.

"Calm down!" she shouted at him.

"Heather! Please!" He made another grab.

"Calm down, you idiot! It *wasn't her!*" she screamed at him.

Those were the magic words. Sam stopped moving finally. In his beautiful hazel eyes Heather saw so much hope and relief, she thought she might throw up.

Sam took a breath. "What did you say?"

Heather didn't try to hide the disgust in her face. And Sam was so far away, he didn't seem to see it or care. "I said, it wasn't her. It wasn't Gaia," Heather repeated flatly.

"Are you sure?" Sam asked, his eyes too vulnerable for words.

Heather couldn't help wondering, in a profoundly awful way, whether anybody, *anybody* would ever care about her as much as Sam seemed to care for Gaia right now.

Real rage began smoldering in her stomach. Couldn't he at least *pretend* he didn't adore Gaia so deeply? Couldn't he consider

Heather for *one single second* and attempt to spare her feelings? "I'm sure," she spat out bitterly.

"Oh," he said.

Finally he brought his eyes back to Heather. He seemed to remember she was in the room with him. He took another few breaths. He looked tentative. He was ashamed. But more than that, more than anything, he was relieved that cut-up girl wasn't his beloved Gaia.

In one quiet moment everything was clear. They'd both known the truth long before this. Sam was obsessed with Gaia.

Heather was too hurt to feel it. Her heart was on autopilot once more. "You've fallen for her, haven't you?" Her voice was empty.

Sam ran a hand through his hair, leaving most of it standing straight up. He looked down at the floor, then back to Heather's eyes. "I guess I have." His voice was so quiet, he mouthed the words as much as said them.

At least he didn't lie or try to bullshit her, she told herself. His honesty made for cold comfort, though.

"I don't know why. I'm so sorry," he finished earnestly.

She hated him.

"Don't apologize," she snapped icily. "Just . . . get out of here. I don't want to see you right now. We'll talk about it some other time." Anger was accessible to her right now. Pain was not.

Numbly she strode to the coat closet and grabbed his corduroy jacket. She practically threw it at him. "Please go!"

He looked sorry, all right. Sorry and regretful, but also relieved. So relieved, he was ashamed of himself. He was happy to be getting out of there and away from her.

She hated him.

"I'm sorry, Heather," he said again as he walked out of the apartment. "I'm really sorry."

She hardly waited until he was clear of the door before she slammed it with all her might.

She wheeled around. "I hate you!" she shouted at the empty living room.

For some reason the story of Medea invaded her head again. The bitter, scorned, miserable woman.

Heather went back to the couch and threw all the pillows on the floor. It was lucky for Sam that they didn't have any children.

GRANDPA FARGO'S FAMOUS APPLE PIE

Ingredients:

8 red Rome apples
1 recipe pie crust
$\frac{1}{2}$ cup sugar
$\frac{1}{2}$ teaspoon cinnamon
2 tablespoons flour
pinch of nutmeg
pinch of salt
1 tablespoon butter
1 well-beaten egg

Filling:

Peel and core apples and slice into $\frac{1}{2}$"
wedges. Place in large mixing bowl. Add
sugar, cinnamon, flour, nutmeg, and salt.
Toss until thoroughly blended.
Roll $\frac{1}{2}$ pie crust dough to $\frac{1}{8}$-inch thickness.
Line 9-inch pie plate with dough, allowing $\frac{1}{2}$
inch to extend over edge. Add filling. Dot
with 1 tablespoon butter. Roll out rest of
dough and lay over pie plate, tucking excess
dough along pie-plate edge. Crimp along edge
with knife handle to create a wavy pattern.
Use fork to puncture a few holes into top of
crust in pattern of your choice. Brush top of
pie with 1 well-beaten egg.
Bake at 425 degrees for 15 minutes. Turn
down heat to 350 degrees and bake for $\frac{1}{2}$
hour.

Without
thinking,
she threw
herself on
his **freedom/
nothingness**
bed. It was
sick, but so
delicious.

GREEN. RED. GREEN. RED. OUT the front window of the diner on University Place, Gaia watched the traffic light run its cycle again and again. She thought of Ed.

Wobbly

She'd meant to go, she really had. But here she was again.

She realized she was still shivering. She put her hand to her throbbing head. God, what she would do for a dollar to buy a hot cup of coffee.

"Excuse me, sweetheart, but if you're not going to order anything, I'm going to have to ask you to leave." The waitress wasn't mean. She was old and tired. She had turned a blind eye to Gaia for the last forty-five minutes. Now she was doing her job.

"But it's so cold out," Gaia said, mostly to herself.

"What's that, hon?" The waitress leaned in.

"Nothing, I'm going." It took all of Gaia's strength to climb out of the booth and balance herself on her feet. The room spun around her. She closed her eyes, trying not to be sick.

"Are you okay?" the woman asked.

Gaia opened her eyes. She steadied herself against the top of the vinyl seats. "Yes, I'll be fine," she said. She walked as steadily as she could to the door and steeled herself for the cold blast of wind.

Back out on the street she hugged herself for warmth. She wished she had her coat. She wished she had a blanket. She wished she had anything heavier than this skimpy red dress. And Mary was wrong. These shoes *were* too small. Her feet ached.

She made herself walk. What now? Where could she go? The light to cross Thirteenth Street was red. To cross to the west side of University was green. She crossed.

She kept walking west. Her teeth chattered uncontrollably. When she got to Fifth Avenue, the light to cross was red. The light to cross Thirteenth to the south was green. She crossed.

The wind that whipped up Fifth Avenue seemed to find its way into her skin—into every muscle and nerve and tendon. It chilled her blood in her veins, and her veins circulated that chilled blood all through her body and into her heart.

The light to cross Twelfth Street was red. The light to cross to the west side of Fifth was green. She crossed. Without instructions her feet were taking her to her home in New York City—Washington Square Park. She crossed Twelfth Street and got another green signal to cross Eleventh. The miniature Arc de Triomphe that marked the northern entrance to the park was in full view now.

She glanced up and stopped. The building to her right was familiar. Familiar mostly in a painful way. It was Sam's dormitory, the place where she'd walked in on Sam and Heather having sex.

She started walking and stopped again. Another image appeared in her mind. The broken doorknob. Too well she remembered the wobbly brass sphere almost falling off in her hand, giving her access to one of the worst sights a person could see. But right now, from where she stood, the broken doorknob held a certain appeal.

SAM FELT DISGUSTINGLY LIGHT ON

his feet as he walked down Third Avenue. He should have been miserable or at least heavyhearted. But he wasn't. His muscles were buzzing with life. The world looked new to him. Clean and fresh and in excellent focus.

Now What?

He looked at the shops on either side of the avenue, closed up for the holiday, with their iron safety gates pulled down and locked. It was the kind of sight that had depressed him when he'd first moved to New York. Tonight he liked it.

He was sorry about Heather. He was sorry *for* Heather. He genuinely was. She didn't deserve to be treated the way she'd been treated. But nor did she deserve to have a boyfriend who thought so constantly of someone else.

And now, for the first time in months, he felt free. Free for the moment, anyway.

Free to be with Gaia, a voice in his mind added.

Hold up, he ordered that voice. He wasn't sure about anything yet. He wasn't sure what the real status was between him and Heather. He wasn't sure whether Gaia had ever looked at him the way he looked at her.

Most importantly, Gaia was a major proposition. For him, he knew, she represented a love-of-his-life possibility. He had to be slow. He had to be careful. He had to make sure he didn't somehow get killed in the process.

He stopped at a red light. His happy legs had covered a lot of ground without him even knowing it. Now where?

He imagined his dorm room. It would be so lonely tonight. The place would be absolutely deserted. But where else could he go? All his friends were back home or visiting relatives. He imagined his family back in Maryland. His older brother was bringing his new girlfriend home to meet the folks. His parents were sorry that he wasn't there, and now, the way things had turned out, so was he.

His mind turned to Gaia, as it often did. Where was she spending Thanksgiving? She didn't have parents; that was one of the few things he knew about her. A very sad circumstance on a day like this. Did she like the Nivens, those people she lived with? Was she in their house on Perry Street right now? Was she happy? On some level he knew she wasn't, and that gave him a deep, achy feeling he didn't often feel for another person.

Why did he care for her like this? How had it happened?

He saw the lights of an all-night diner burning up ahead. It was one of the few establishments open along the whole avenue. Maybe he'd duck in there. Find himself a copy of *The New York Times* and while away the evening with a couple of cups of coffee.

THERE IS NO WAY SAM COULD BE

here, Gaia told herself for the tenth time. She was certain of it. Sam was the kind of guy who had a loving family and scores of other good backup options for Thanksgiving in case the family thing wasn't happening. In fact, he was probably sharing warm food and feelings with the she-wolf.

The Key

Still, Gaia felt self-conscious as she stepped into the

entrance of the NYU dorm. She was tired of looking like a prostitute in this awful dress. The place was nearly deserted but for the omnipresent security guard at a table a few yards into the lobby. Shit, she'd forgotten about him. He was absorbed in a noisy hockey game playing on the tiny TV perched on the table less than a foot from his eyes.

The warm air felt so good. If she could just manage to stay in here for a few minutes, maybe she'd be okay. Now that she'd finally slowed her pace, the dizziness was coming back.

The guard and his TV were in their own little world. Maybe she could just . . .

"Excuse me? Uh, miss? Can I help you?" Damn. There must have been a time-out in the game or something. The security guard was now staring at her with his full attention.

"H-Hi. I j-just. Um. My f-f-friend lives here, and he inv-v-vited me over," Gaia said. She was shivering so hard, it was difficult to talk.

The security guard got a knowing look in his eyes. "Hey, I'm sorry, sweetheart, but we can't have none of that here." He took in her slinky, ripped dress, her heels, what was left of her makeup. "This is a college building, you know? You oughtta get out of here." He kept jingling his keys in one hand. It seemed like a nervous habit. She noticed that the key ring said Mustang and showed the black silhouette of a horse bucking against a blue background.

"B-B-But I—" Gaia knew there was really no point in arguing. There was no way he was letting her past his table unless she clobbered him, and she simply didn't have the strength. She just wanted to use up a little more time inside. She couldn't face the cold again. What could she talk about with him? The New York Rangers? Cars? Guns?

"Look, kid, I'm sorry. I really am. You look like hell"—he shook his head with a mix of sympathy and disgust—"but you can't stay here."

SAM TOOK OUT HIS WALLET SOON

after he'd sat down at a table to see how much cash he had. He rifled through every compartment. Unfortunately, he had none. He checked the pockets of his jacket. He had no money. Not one red cent.

He remembered now that he'd given Heather two twenties to buy pies for dessert from an overpriced Upper East Side gourmet shop.

150

He flagged down a waiter. "Excuse me, do you take credit cards?"

The surly waiter fixed him with a look that clearly meant no.

"Do you know if there's a bank or an ATM around here?" he asked.

The waiter looked like Sam had burned his house down. "Twenty-theerd," the man replied in a clipped, Eastern European accent.

"But this is Thirty-first Street," Sam said, wondering why he bothered.

"Twenty-theerd," the waiter said, louder.

Sam blew out his breath. "Okay, thanks." He headed toward the door. It looked like he was going to end up in his dorm room after all.

AS SHE LEFT THE DORMITORY, THE

Moony cold practically knocked Gaia senseless. She was covered head to toe in goose bumps, only they didn't seem the least bit compelling.

Suddenly, a few yards from the building, she stopped. Her eye caught on a logo on the hood of a car parked directly outside the dorm's entrance.

So she wasn't totally senseless. She walked slowly

around the car, studying it for another moment. Then she saw the vanity license plate. RANGER-FAN, it read. Oh God. Could it be? Could there actually be a small piece of good luck in all of this blackness?

Gaia put her hands to her head. She needed to expel the dizziness, to gather her wits and her physical capabilities if she had any left.

Okay, now. She raised her foot to the side of the hood and shoved it hard. The car rocked violently, and a car alarm blasted through the silent night air. Perfect.

She ran to the side of the building and backed herself up against the wall, a few feet beyond the front awning.

Exactly as she'd hoped, the security guard dashed out of the building to check on his precious vehicle. Thank God.

Gaia found enough speed left in her legs to carry her into the building, undetected. With excitement fizzing in her veins she sprinted into the stairwell and up four flights to the door of Sam's suite.

She slowed down. Okay, this was starting to bring back some bad memories. Still, it was warm. There was a bed. She had to put her emotions on ice for a while.

Slowly she opened the door to the common room of the suite, blanking out her mind. Good, it was empty. The door to room B5, with its infamous doorknob, was just ahead.

Please be broken still, she begged of the doorknob. She closed her eyes and closed her hand around it at the same time.

Yes. She let out a breath. It jiggled brokenly in its socket, and she was able to push open the door.

Icy as her emotions—and the rest of her—were, she wasn't prepared for the effect of the smell. The tiny dorm room smelled like Sam. In a good way. In an aching, moony, grab-you-by-the-heart way. The smell intoxicated her. It gave her shivers. Why was it that a smell could evoke a person more powerfully than a million pictures could?

This, she realized, was what people meant when they talked about chemistry.

Without thinking, she threw herself on his bed. It was sick, but so delicious. His bed. Where he slept. She imagined him in his boxers, tangled in the sheets. His shoulders, his torso, his stomach, his . . . God, what heady torture.

She sat up. She had to pull herself together. She was semidemented from bashing her head and from cold and exhaustion. Time to act like a sane person.

First thing was to get out of this dress. She pulled it over her head in one swift move. She pulled the shoes off her miserable feet and stripped off the tights. She wound up the dress, the shoes, and the tights in a ball and sank them into the wastebasket next to Sam's nightstand.

Shower. She needed a shower. She wanted a boiling hot shower so bad, she could feel it.

Aha. There was a towel hanging over the door of Sam's closet. On his bureau were a bar of soap and a bottle of shampoo. Eureka. She had to hope that this dorm really was as empty as it appeared.

She cast off her bra and panties, feeling an unfamiliar and lustful pleasure at seeing them strewn about on Sam's bed. She wrapped herself in the towel and set off in search of the bathroom.

She listened for the sound of the germs, and they led her to a totally filthy and wonderful bathroom off the common room. What could you ask from a bathroom shared by four college students? She didn't care. She loved every microbe.

She blasted the shower as hot and strong as it would go and climbed in.

She gathered sex felt pretty good, but she couldn't imagine it felt much better than hot jets of water pounding against her frozen flesh. Ahhhhhh.

Suddenly the tiles were starting a slow spin around her. She pressed her palms into her eyeballs. It didn't help. She sat right down on the floor of the shower and let the water beat down on her head. She would wait for the dizziness to pass.

When her body finally felt warm from the outside in, she got back to her feet and scrubbed her hair and face and body and rinsed for ages. She had to force herself to turn off the water.

She wrapped herself in Sam's towel and crept back into his room. Now what? Should she sleep naked or should she . . . hmmm. She went over to Sam's bureau and opened the top drawer. Waiting for her there were a soft, clean, ribbed white tank top undershirt and a pair of well-worn cotton boxers in a faded plaid of blues and greens. Yum.

This night had turned from sheer torment to the most sensual and thrilling experience of her life. She felt a bit like a stalker, but she wasn't doing any harm, was she? She'd put everything back in order before Sam returned. He'd never even guess she was there.

On the floor at the foot of his bed she suddenly spied his shoes, the scuffed leather, lace-up shoes he'd been wearing the day they played chess. For some reason, the sight of them stole her breath. Though empty, the shoes sat in a pose that was strongly suggestive of Sam—of exactly how he stood and walked. It was crazy that a pair of uninhabited shoes could carry so much subtle information about him. But they did. They brought him right into the room with her.

The aching feeling was back in force. She shivered again. An army of goose bumps invaded her arms and legs and back. *Almost like fear.*

It was like fear, but it wasn't fear.

Maybe it was . . . love.

Dear Gaia,

I made a decision today, a few hours after you left. I'm going straight—I'm giving up drugs. Not "one day at a time" or any of that crap. I'm giving it up for good. Right now. When you saw me snorting coke today, I saw myself through your eyes, and I hated what I saw. If I keep going like this, I'm going to die. Yeah, it's that bad. And I don't want to die yet.

You probably wish I'd just leave you alone. You're wondering why I'm dragging you into my problems. I'm not sure, exactly. I'm not a very reflective person. But for some reason, I really do want to be friends with you. I want to be close. (Don't worry. Not in that way. I'm not a lesbian.) I've made a specialty out of not caring what other people think. But I do care what you think. I want you to think I'm a good person.

I have this idea about you and me. I have everything—parents, money, friends, a lot of love. You have nothing. I get so much, and the thing that sucks is, my heart is like a sieve. I want you to have some of what I have. You deserve it, not me.

That's weird, right? Sorry, it's just how I am.

So, anyway, I'm kicking the drugs whether I ever see you again or not.

But I just wanted you to know that wherever you are,

however you feel, you always have a friend out there in the world. Not a perfect friend or anything, but one who's trying to do better.

Mary

Mary finished the letter and stuck it in an envelope. She'd get a stamp from her mom later. Then she got an idea. She went to her desk drawer, where she'd had a one-pound bag of M&M's ever since Halloween. She dumped the entire contents on her floor and picked out every last one of the red ones. She transferred the letter into a bigger, sturdier envelope and threw in all of the red M&M's to keep it company. She threw in a few green ones, too.

Now she'd need a whole bunch of stamps.

He was
leaning
forward,
leaning
over her. So
close now.
So real.
"Can I?" he
whispered.

the color of love

"HEY, BAUMAN, WHAT'S UP?" SAM said to the security guard. "How're the Rangers?"

Something Sublime

Bauman grimaced. "Down by two in the third. How's your holiday, Moon?"

Sam actually thought about his answer. "Good," he said. "Surprisingly good." Except for the fact that all twenty digits had lost feeling about a mile ago. He rubbed his hands together. "Quiet here tonight, huh?"

"Yes, it is," Bauman answered vaguely, his attention back on the game.

"Later. Happy Thanksgiving," Sam called over his shoulder as he entered the stairwell. Not that he expected his bland sign-off to compete with the Rangers. He was pathologically polite. He couldn't help himself.

He took the stairs slowly. Was he the only student in the entire building? It felt almost eerie.

None of his suite mates were around, that much he knew. He swung open the door of the common room. The place was exactly the pigsty he'd left it. He didn't even bother to turn on a light. He'd so completely frozen himself, walking almost seventy blocks, he was eager to strip down and climb under his down comforter.

He took out his key and had started to fit it in the

lock when the doorknob fell off in his hand. "Shit. Gotta get that fixed," he cursed under his breath, as he did two out of three times he entered his room.

A warm, reddish light from the street was filtering through the small window, lighting the bed. . . .

Oh. Jesus. Sam stepped backward. He was suddenly transported to a Three Little Bears moment. There was someone sleeping in his bed.

He stepped forward and froze. His heart stopped beating. He stopped breathing. Brain function shut down.

Could that someone be . . . ?

He turned his eyes to the door and then back to the bed again, sure that the mirage would be gone. It wasn't. There was still a sublimely beautiful blond girl in his bed who looked very much like Gaia.

He'd heard that people hallucinated in the happiest way just before they died of exposure. He hadn't chilled himself that badly, had he?

Now. Time to breathe, lungs. Time to beat, heart. His vital organs appeared to need a little coaching. There. Better. Okay, deep breaths. Yes.

He would just calm down, slow down, and think a minute.

He crept a little closer, terrified that this magnificent vision would disappear if he disturbed the air the slightest bit.

Still there. Please stay, he begged it. If this was a

161

figment of his imagination, then he prayed his imagination would keep it up.

He would just look at her. That would be okay, wouldn't it? Even if it was an imagined version of her, he still wanted to look. The few interactions he and Gaia'd had were so charged or awkward or plain antagonistic that he never got to study her, to see how her face looked in repose.

Her head was turned to the side, and her silken yellow hair—hair he'd fantasized about more times than was good for him—was splayed out on the pillow, leaving a shadow of dampness on the white cotton. Her bewitching eyes were closed in sleep. Her face was serene and lovely beyond description—light freckles over her cheeks. He drew closer. Palest, finest down along her jawline. Her eyelids flickered. He drew back.

She was still again. He came closer. His eyes moved down her neck.

Oh Christ! She was wearing his T-shirt. He felt the blood churning in his ears, gathering in other parts of his body. His T-shirt, which had spent its long, dutiful life covering large, rough stretches of masculine skin, now had the exquisite experience of gracing skin so delicate and fine, it was almost transparent. He envied it.

He saw that the too large shirt had gotten pulled around under her, revealing the sloping side and top of her breast.

He had to look away. Partly because it was too much to take and partly because he felt wrong seeing her like this, without her knowing he was seeing her. Without her wanting him to.

He made himself take a few steps backward and put his hands over his face to regain his composure.

He knew now, more than ever before, that he loved her. He loved her deeply and urgently, with a fierceness that made him know he'd never grasped, even grazed, the concept of love before. But he couldn't go on like this, without knowing how she really felt.

And what if she wasn't real at all but a figment of his fevered, lustful mind?

Well, then she'd be more likely to tell him what he dreamed of hearing.

GAIA WAS DREAMING A BLISSFUL

dream. Surrounded as she was by the smell and feel of Sam, by his place and his things, it was natural that she should dream of him vividly.

In the dream he was there beside her, sitting on the edge of the bed. He was so close, she could feel his warmth and smell his smell more intensely. An alive smell now.

He took her hand so gently and held it. Just held it. Making her safe.

Consciousness was tickling her eyelids, summoning her. *Please, sleep, stay with me. Don't make me go back yet.*

But it was happening. She couldn't help it. She was waking up in spite of every effort to fight it. She flicked open her eyes.

No.

She closed them again.

How could it be?

She opened them again. Was the dream still with her? . . . Or was it . . .

"Sam?" she whispered, her heart filled with awe.

He was still holding her hand. In the dream and . . . here. He was still holding it, one of his hands cupping her fingers, the other holding her wrist. His beautiful hands with the wide nails and fraying cuticles. The ones he'd used to stomp all over her chess pieces that day in the park when this had started.

"Gaia," he said. She'd never heard her name sound just that way before.

He was leaning forward, leaning over her. So close now. So real. "Can I?" he whispered.

"Please," she said.

He took his hand from her wrist and touched his first two fingers to her elbow, then drew them in an air-light caress up to her shoulder. "Mmmm," she sighed.

As his head hovered over her she looked up at his neck and chin, touching her finger to the place where his whiskers started, moving them up over his jaw, feeling the slight hollow of his cheek, the strong bones that came together at the corner of his eye. He gazed down at her, his eyes voracious and questioning. She turned her head to face him straight on.

"Oh," he said, drawing in his breath. He touched his fingers to the ugly bruise along the side of her cheek and forehead. His face showed real worry. "Are you okay?"

She felt like crying just then. She'd forgotten about everything that had happened. Now she remembered, and she felt ashamed of it and of all the ugliness and violence she represented in Sam's good, peaceful life. "I'm sorry," she said randomly, her eyes filling with tears.

"No, Gaia," he whispered. "Don't. Just . . . be with me."

The feelings inside her were too round and full. She couldn't hold them. Her chest was bursting, and her head was spinning.

He pulled her up so she was sitting beside him and gently held her face in her hands. He put his lips, gentle as sunlight, to the wound on her forehead, then dotted her cheekbone with kisses.

Please, please, please, she begged silently. Wishing.

Oh God. And then he found it, and her wish happened. His lips found her mouth, and the gentleness gave way to intensity. A kiss. A real kiss more perfect than any imagined. She was kissing him back, hungrily, pressing herself against him.

A thought came to her as his lips melted into hers. *This*, she thought, *is the mouth that I was meant to kiss. This is the mouth I will always kiss, and no other.* And blending into that thought was another thought. More a feeling than a thought, because there were no words to it at all. But the feeling was that her lips and her hands had found a home. The one safe, healing place on earth. And that maybe, maybe . . . who could ever say? But maybe she really would have kids someday. (Not just one.) Because there was somebody in the world for her. She knew that now, from this kiss, and nobody could take that away.

His hands held the back of her head now; they were buried in her hair. His lips explored hers. She tasted him and felt him and smelled him all at once. Her senses mixed and blurred. Her blood roared in her ears.

He stood up and pulled her with him. He pressed the entire length of his body against her. She tilted back her head, not wanting to break the kiss. She let her hands explore his graceful, muscular back, his wide, sturdy shoulders. She touched his neck and felt the way his hair curled sweetly around his ears. Digging her fingers into his hair, she pushed him deeper, harder into the kiss.

He moaned. His arms were around her now, gathering her up, holding her as tight and close against him as she could be and still remain a separate person. His lips left hers, landing under her jaw, down her neck, her collarbone.

"Aaaaaah." A breathy sound escaped her lips. The dizziness was overpowering; it was shutting her in. These feelings were too fragile and beautiful to be held, the love too big to fit into her scarred, shrunken heart.

"I love you." Did she think it, or did she say it? Or did he say it? Or did she imagine he said it? Were the words in the air or just in her mind?

Before she could be sure, the darkness engulfed her, and she released herself to the sureness of Sam's arms.

"I LOVE YOU," SAM WHISPERED

Siren Song

against her neck. "I love you."

He'd always wondered what it would take to say those words, how much he'd have to push and prompt and coach himself to utter them. He didn't realize it wouldn't require any intention at all—that the words could come without thought or plan, as naturally and passionately and irreversibly as a kiss, without waiting for his consent.

Suddenly he felt her weight sink into his arms.

"Gaia." He pulled her up to him, finding her face with his lips, kissing her eyelids. They were closed. "Gaia?"

Her eyes didn't open. She breathed a sigh. Her head fell forward, resting against his chest. "Gaia?"

He cradled her head in the crook of his elbow and tipped her back gently. "Gaia? Are you all right? Gaia?"

She had fainted. She was motionless in his arms. All the feelings whirring in his chest changed directions, from pure exultation to surprise and fear.

He picked her up in his arms, cradling her against him. "Gaia. Gaia!" He jostled her, hoping to rouse her. Her head fell back, `exposing her delicate throat.`

"Gaia, please? What happened? Are you okay?" Panic was building. His eyes found the terrible bruise on the side of her head. Could it be . . . ? What if . . . ?

"Gaia, come on. Stay with me here, would you? Please, Gaia." The fear was talking. He was listening only distractedly.

He managed to support her weight with one arm and with the other plucked the phone from his nightstand. He dialed 911.

"Thirty-two Fifth!" he blared into the phone as soon as he heard a voice pick up. "Fourth floor. Send an ambulance."

"Sir, can you tell me what has happened?" the voice urged calmly.

"M-My . . . girlfriend." (Girlfriend?) "She's fainted. I can't rouse her. She hurt her head. Maybe—"

"All right, sir, we'll send the ambulance immediately."

Sam's heart was slamming in his rib cage. Thoughts were careening around his brain like a million errant Ping-Pong balls. "Oh, Gaia, please be okay," he begged her still body.

He laid her down as gingerly as he could on his bed. It was cold out. He needed to cover her. Did she have clothes or . . . ? No time.

He grabbed his thick, terry cloth robe from his closet and wrapped her in it. It was a strange set of circumstances that would force him to willingly cover her magnificent body, not to let his eyes linger over her exquisite stomach and hips and legs.

He found a wool blanket on the shelf and bundled her in that, too. Then he scooped her lifeless body up and strode out into the hallway. He punched the button for the elevator, his ears pricked for the sound of a siren. It was the one time he invited that sound, desperately wanted to hear it.

The elevator came. Sam stabbed at the lobby button.

There it was! The siren! Thank the Lord for a quick response. He raced past a stunned-looking Bauman and met the ambulance just as it was pulling up outside.

Fear blended with appreciation as Sam watched

the emergency medical team burst into action, their limbs and instruments a blur of confidence and precision. He loved them in that moment as much as he loved his parents and friends.

Before a minute had passed, Gaia was bound in a stretcher, hooked up to various medical gadgets, tucked into the back of the vehicle with Sam beside her. The engine roared, the siren kicked in again, and they were off to St. Vincent's, just a few blocks away.

Sam held her hand tight, never wanting to let it go.

"I love you," he whispered to her again, pleading with his crazed heart to stay in his chest for a while longer.

He considered it for a moment, his newly awakened heart. He remembered the puzzling conflict between heart and mind. Well, it was settled now.

In case there was any mystery, he now knew who was in charge.

GAIA WAS FLOATING. SAM WAS there, holding her hand. There were unfamiliar people, sounds, words, things she couldn't make sense of, but there was always Sam. He held her. He gave her his warmth.

Heaven

"I love you." The words came to her in Sam's voice. She wanted very much to open her eyes and see if it really was Sam, and if so, to see if he was talking to her when he said them, as she fervently hoped he was. And if he was saying those words to her, and maybe even if he wasn't, she wanted to say the same words to him.

But she couldn't. She couldn't open her eyes or make words.

Was she alive anymore? Was Sam real? Was he really there with her?

Maybe it was him. More likely it was heaven.

But if this was heaven, if this was what death felt like, then it was okay with her.

I've been trying to figure
out why I don't have any tears
for Sam tonight.

I do hate him at the moment;
that's true.

But I thought I loved him.

All this time I figured I
haven't been able to cry over him
because I'm too numb. I'm too
bottled up and confused to feel
things very well.

I never imagined the possibility that I didn't love him.

Because I do love him. I mean,
I'm pretty sure I do.

I mean, I do. Don't I?

You know what's really re-
tarded? An hour after Sam left, I
called Ed Fargo.

Then I remembered he was in
Pennsylvania. He was there for
Thanksgiving with his weird,
obese grandmother who called me
Feather.

Then the
memories
fell into
fragments
and shards
that **hunger**
didn't make
any sense at
all.

ELLA ROLLED HER EYES AT THE

emergency-room doctor in St. Vincent's Hospital. This was a night of highs and lows, currently stuck on low.

More Disappointment

The doctor was talking about Gaia, bleating words like *concussion* and *subdural* something and *hematoma* something else. But he wasn't saying anything about "slashed to ribbons," which was what Ella really wanted to hear.

She was jubilant when she'd first gotten the call from the hospital, sure that her plans had gone off without a hitch. Then she entered a period of confusion after she arrived at the hospital, during which it appeared that Gaia *hadn't* been slashed at Penn Station. Gaia, she was told, had spent several semidelirious hours before a doting Sam Moon brought her to the hospital, unconscious, from his NYU dormitory. The girl who'd been slashed (Ella had followed the story excitedly on the eleven o'clock news) was *not* Gaia, and yet Gaia had found her way to the hospital with some grave problem nonetheless.

Ella perked up when she heard the doctor use the

word *coma,* hoping that her goal might be achieved even without the extra bonus of disfigurement. But `wretched, impossible Gaia` had miraculously managed to sidestep the coma, in spite of a serious head injury.

"Mrs. Niven, I'm sorry to bother you with all of this information. I'm sure you'd like to see her," Dr. Somethingorother was saying. He was Indian or maybe Pakistani and spoke precise, melodious English.

Ella sighed. She couldn't very well say no, could she? "Of course," she said.

"You'll be pleased to know she's already been moved out of ICU. Her condition is stable."

Whoopee.

Ella followed the white coat up an elevator and down a hallway, through a set of swinging doors, past a waiting room and a nurses' station.

Dr. Whatever turned around to talk some more. "She's not yet fully conscious. Still a bit bleary. Try not to be alarmed. We do expect her to make a quick recovery, but it's never as quick as all of us would like."

`If Gaia woke up before she was thirty, it would be too quick.` Ella nodded blandly. She hated doctors. Particularly the one she'd blown up earlier in the evening.

The doctor stopped in front of room 448. The

door was partially open. He gestured for her to enter first. She started into the room and quickly stepped backward. She backed out into the hallway.

"Excuse me, Doctor," she said. "But there's somebody else in the room."

The doctor's eyes lit up. "Yes, that's her friend who brought her here. His name is Sam, I think? He hasn't left her side in hours. He is quite devoted to her, no? He is the one who gave us the information to find you."

"Fine," she said. "Very nice. But would you mind asking him to leave? I really need some time alone with my . . . foster daughter." Sob, sob. "Besides," she added in a confidential tone, "if I can speak frankly, I don't like that young man. I wouldn't be surprised if he were part of the reason that Gaia is here in the first place. . . ." She let her voice float off enigmatically.

The doctor hesitated. Clearly he didn't know what to think, and yet he was too polite to question her. "Yes. As you wish," he said.

"I'll just use the bathroom and collect myself for a moment," Ella said, stepping down the hall. "I'll come back when I can see Gaia alone."

A strong instinct was telling Ella she didn't want to be introduced to Sam Moon. A somewhat twisted instinct, but those were the ones she'd learned to listen to.

SAM WATCHED GAIA'S EYELIDS

One Witness

for signs of her waking. Just in the last five minutes she'd opened and closed her eyes three times, once almost focusing on his face. His heart soared. Dr. Sengupta said she was going to be okay, and he was starting to believe it.

Sam ran his thumb from the tip of her index finger up her hand and wrist to the soft underside of her forearm. Her eyes flickered.

He leaned over her and buried a gentle kiss on her neck. That was more for him than her. He hoped she didn't mind. The hint of a smile seemed to pull at the side of her mouth. Or did he just imagine that?

What he really wanted to do was to climb into the narrow bed and press her close to him, to hold her with his whole body until she woke up. And after she woke up, too. But you weren't really supposed to do that in a hospital, were you?

Most people hated hospitals, and in theory, Sam did, too. But this hospital, on two separate occasions, had brought him closer to Gaia. It was the site of some of his worst experiences and yet some of the happiest feelings he'd ever had.

"Sam?"

He glanced up. He saw Gaia's doctor and felt slightly abashed. "Yes?"

"I'm sorry to ask you because I can see how much you wish to stay with Gaia, but her guardian, Mrs. Niven, has asked for time alone with her."

Sam knew it was a reasonable request, but his heart was breaking nonetheless. "Maybe I'll just wait in the waiting room for a few minutes till she's done."

Dr. Sengupta took in the state of Sam's hair and clothing with kind eyes. "Why don't you get yourself home and have a rest? Perhaps you could come again tomorrow? Visiting hours, as you might imagine, are long over."

Visiting hours? Sam was no visitor! He was . . . what? Nothing. He was nothing. But `Gaia was his life.` Did that count for anything?

"But I—" He really, really didn't want to go yet. He wanted to help usher Gaia back into the land of consciousness, to be with her when she crossed over. He needed to make sure they both knew that what happened between them was real. "Please, could I just—"

"I'm sorry. I have to respect Mrs. Niven's request." The doctor did look truly sorry.

Sam turned back to Gaia. He took both of her hands and brought them to his heart. He leaned over and pressed his cheek against her good one. "I love you, Gaia," he whispered in her ear. "I can't help it anymore." It might not have been a classically romantic thing to say, but it was true. She'd understand, he knew. He kissed her ear, then straightened up.

Her eyelids were fluttering again. He saw her hands moving against the sheet as soon as he'd released them. Were her hands looking for his? Did he just hope so?

"Thank you, Doctor, for everything," he said, trying not to look as unhappy as he felt. "She's really going to be okay, right?"

"Yes, I believe she is."

Sam trudged out of the room and down the hallway.

"Good luck to you, Sam," the doctor called after him, and the words somehow sounded ominous.

Every cell in Sam's heart was telling him not to leave her now. He was afraid that once he was gone, their magical, frightening night together would be gone, too, with him left as its only witness.

And not the most reliable witness, either.

IT WAS HARD AND CRUEL. IT

Disappointment x 1,000,000,000

downright sucked. In her dream, hovering someplace beyond the living, Gaia had Sam. He held her and told her he loved her.

Here, in reality, she had Ella.

She wished she could go back to being dead.

". . . You have quite a track record, Gaia. Twice in the hospital in two months," Ella was blathering. "You're going to send George's insurance premiums into the stratosphere."

Gaia exerted all her strength propping herself up in the hospital bed. It made her uncomfortable for Ella to see her lying down.

". . . And insurance only covers eighty percent of the bill, you know," Ella continued pettily.

Gaia looked down at her hands. They felt cold and lonely. "Thanks a lot, Ella," she said numbly. "That makes me feel a lot better. If the photography thing doesn't work out, maybe you could get a job with Hallmark in the get-well-card department."

Ella exhaled in annoyance. "And you're a rude ingrate as well."

Gaia closed her eyes, wrapping her misery around her like a blanket. She was right back where she started. She'd thought she'd made a new friend. She hadn't. She'd thought she'd run away. She hadn't.

She'd gotten nowhere, changed nothing.

Her mind summoned an image of Sam. She was kissing him, touching him, wrapping her body around his in his bed. The image brought a deep flush to her cheeks. But that hadn't really . . . They hadn't actually . . . had they?

She glanced at Ella.

What exactly *had* happened to her? How had she gotten here? She tried to piece together the endless, surreal day. She remembered being at Mary's house, of course. She remembered hitting her head on the sink in the bathroom at Penn Station. She remembered passing out—if you could call that remembering.

Things got fuzzier after that. She didn't remember coming to, but she did remember trying to get a refund for her stolen ticket. She vaguely remembered an explosion. She remembered walking outside and being cold.

Then the memories fell into fragments and shards that didn't make any sense at all.

She glanced at Ella again. She could hardly stomach the notion of needing information from the bitch goddess, but how else was she going to know?

Gaia took a breath. She needed to sound as disinterested as possible. "So, anyway, Ella. What happened to me? How did I get here? How did you get here?"

Ella opened her eyes wide in fake surprise. "Wait a minute. You are asking *me* questions about *your* life?"

Gaia shrugged. "You know, severe head wound and all." She touched her hand to her bruise. "I just wondered if the doctors told you anything about how I ended up here."

Ella studied her for a moment. "Actually, yes. Do you really not remember anything at all?"

Gaia shook her head. "Not much."

Ella nodded slowly. "Well, you made quite a little scene. The cops found you outside an NYU dormitory. You were delirious, totally out of it, raving endlessly about somebody named Sam."

Gaia felt her heart clench. The flush returned to her cheeks and deepened by one hundred times. If she'd really believed she'd made her heart tough enough to withstand disappointment, she'd been badly, profoundly mistaken.

"I was alone?" Gaia asked in a small voice, even though she knew she'd regret it. "I came here alone?" She was so far gone, she was giving evil Ella a straight shot at her vulnerability.

"Except for some freaked-out cops, yeah," Ella informed her.

So Gaia's fragments of memory weren't memory at all. They were fantasy. Sam hadn't kissed her, held her, told her he loved her. Those were the crazed delusions of her bashed-in head and her pitiful, hungry heart.

She was tempted to bash her head again, to return to the place where she'd had those feelings. Of course they didn't happen in reality. Not in her reality, anyway. It was too nice, too purely good to have happened in her life.

Gaia lay back again. Ella didn't matter. Nothing mattered.

Her misery wasn't a blanket. It was a `strait-jacket` fastened way too tight, threatening to squeeze out her last bit of hope.

I had a terrible thought when I woke up this morning in the bed that Gaia and I had shared, briefly, last night.

I had the thought that I dreamed the whole thing.

I would have stuck with the thought, but I smelled Gaia's faint, sweet smell in my bed. I found more than one long blond hair on my pillow. I found a somewhat tattered red dress and shoes balled up in my garbage can. I confirmed that my under-shirt and boxers were, in fact, missing.

Then I had a fear that was worse than the thought. I was afraid that it had actually hap-pened, but that Gaia wasn't there. I mean, her body was there. But she was so badly hurt and delirious, and practically comatose, that everything I imag-ined between us happened to me. Only to me.

This fear makes me physically sick because I hate the thought of having taken advantage of her in some way.

Selfishly, that's not even the very worst part. Even worse, I fear I've opened my stubborn, tyrannical heart to an event—a girl—so stunning and miraculous, I've even gotten my brain to join in on the thrill of it. Only to discover that it never actually happened.

Which could make a man feel like a creep and a big, pathetic fool.

My brain, not surprisingly, is threatening a very sour "I told you so."

That's the fear, anyway. I'm not sure it's the truth.

But I can say this. I never understood loneliness until I woke up in my bed without her this morning.

Maybe Ella was telling me
the truth. Maybe I was discovered
by the cops, raving outside of
Sam's dormitory, and taken to the
hospital alone.

But when I stepped out of the
hospital bed after my night of
observation and walked my bleary
self into the bathroom, I discovered something peculiar. Under my
hospital robe, I was wearing a
man's undershirt and a man's boxers. These are things I know I do
not own. I don't care how hard I
banged my head.

At the back of the boxers,
just under the waistband,
scrawled in permanent black
marker are two wonderful words.
Can you guess them?

1. Sam
2. Moon

These pieces of physical evi-
dence happen to fit with some
memory shards I have—fuzzy, I'll
admit. I have bits of memories of
being in Sam's dorm room, and
putting those things on.

I'm not saying Sam definitely kissed me. I'm not saying he told me he loved me or anything like that.

I'm just saying, maybe Ella was wrong. Maybe she lied. Maybe.

In all honesty, I don't even want to find out for sure. I want to hold onto these pieces of memory—hopes, if you want to be a killjoy. I can't bear to discover these things didn't happen. I need to cling to the possibility that they did.

Because even the *possibility* of something so beautiful could sustain a heart as desolate as mine for a long, long time.

here is a
sneak peek of
Fearless™ #6:
PAYBACK

There was something very satisfying about hearing them scream. He usually let them get out one, good, loud one before he covered their mouths. No one ever responded to one quick scream. They wrote it off as playing. Or a spider sighting. Or crying wolf.

And he so loved the scream.

It made him feel alive. It pumped him up.

It made the sex so much better.

He sat down on his floor and pulled out his black lock box from beneath his bed, flying through the combination with a quick three flicks of the wrist. Inside was his prized possession. The only thing he'd ever had worth locking up.

His journal. His list. His conquests.

He pulled out the tattered book with its dog-eared pages and cloth cover that was just starting to pull away from the cardboard beneath. Soon it would be time for a new book. But it would be so hard to let this one go. It was like an old friend. It knew all his secrets. All his successes. All his triumphs.

Turning to the first blank page, he rolled the end of his pen around inside his mouth, carefully composing his opening. This wasn't just a place to brag. It was literature. One day, when he was long gone, people would read these pages and know him. Know everything he was.

They would be awed.

He uncapped the pen and started his entry.

Thursday, November 25th. Thanksgiving.

It certainly was a day for giving thanks. And Regina Farrell will thank me one day. When she finally admits to herself that she'll never have anyone better. . . .

Spiky, messy
hair. Sideburns.
Expensive
flannel.

sideburns

Not threatening. **tim**

Definitely not

asking for a

beating.

GAIA STOOD ON LINE IN THE cafeteria on Monday afternoon between two groups of people she couldn't possibly have detested more. The F.O.H.'s (Friends Of Heather) or "foes" as she liked to call them, and the turtleneck-wearing jock-boys. If there was ever a time to cave in to modern

Basic get-away-from-me signals

technology and use a walkman, this was it. Words were being wasted all around her and she would have given anything for a nice pair of headphones and a lot of guitar-type noise.

"Omigod!" one foe squealed. "You totally should have been at CBGB's last night. The hottest guy opened for Fearless. He was like a Lenny-Rob hybrid."

"Not possible," foe number two said, sniffing a bowl of Jell-O in a perfect imitation of a rabbit, and replacing the bowl on the counter. "God couldn't possibly have blessed anyone with genes like that."

"He's playing again in two weeks," said foe number three, the one with the biggest hair ever to spring from a scalp. "Come and see for yourself."

"I am so there," foe number two promised, placing her nearly empty tray in front of the register. "*I* was at the Melody last night and you . . ."

1

Foe number one trailed off as she glanced in Gaia's direction and noticed her not staring. Her top lip actually curled up and she huffed as she turned her back on Gaia, adjusting her tight leather jacket.

"Do you *see* what she's eating?" foe number one sneered. All three foes turned to glare at Gaia's tray. Meatballs. Mashed potatolike substance. Bowl of Jell-O not sniffed by foe number two. Roll with tons of butter patties.

"Do you want some creamed corn, hon?" the lunch lady asked with a pleasant voice.

"Yeah," Gaia answered, mostly to disgust the foes. It worked. They all exchanged a very unoriginal look of grossed-outedness, paid for their food and scurried away.

"There you go, hon," the big lady behind the counter said, heaping on the corn. She smiled at Gaia like she always did and Gaia attempted smiling back. It didn't work, of course, but it was worth the try. Every student in this school might hate her, but at least she was universally loved by the lunch ladies. Gaia was pretty sure she was the only one who actually ate their food.

Gaia handed the woman at the register a crumpled ball of cash and automatically headed for the table she and Ed usually shared. Back corner, underneath the graph that broke down the four food groups as if they were all still in grade school and needed it color-coded

2

for them. She was about to cut left when someone blocked her path.

This was so not the time for anyone to be starting up with her. Not on a Monday when she hadn't eaten and she'd woken up with a sinus headache along with the knowledge that Sam hadn't contacted her once all weekend.

Actually, maybe someone should start with her. She could go for a little punishment-doling.

"You're a brave girl," a slow, drawly voice said.

Gaia looked up into the deepest pair of brown eyes she'd ever seen. Spiky, messy hair. Sideburns. Expensive flannel. Not threatening. Definitely not asking for a beating.

"Are you going to move?" Gaia asked, shifting her tray slightly. Bad idea. Her plate of meatballs slid precariously close to the edge, taking everything with it. It was going over and there was nothing she could do. More public spillage for the Spillage Queen.

"Careful," Sideburns said, righting the tray with lightning-quick reflexes. The kid in the chair next to them pulled himself a little closer to his table. Gaia attempted to move again, beyond ready to end this little encounter, but Sideburns was still holding onto her tray. "Aren't you going to ask me why I think you're so brave?" he asked, ducking his chin in an attempt to make eye contact. What was this guy's deal? Was he immune to basic get-away-from-me signals?

"No," Gaia said. Exasperation. There. He had to get that.

He released her tray, crossing his arms over his rather broad chest, but not moving out of the way. Gaia turned around to head back in the other direction, but a complicated melange of backpacks, chairs, and legs blocked her path.

When she turned around again, Sideburns was grinning. "It's just that in the three and a third years I've been here I've never seen anyone eat Greta's meatballs."

Oh, how very original. "There's a first time for everything," Gaia said. She took a step toward him, hoping he wasn't going to force her to take him down with a quick flick of her foot to his shin. He seemed harmless enough, but if she didn't eat soon, this Monday was going to go from suckfest to hell pit in a matter of seconds.

Sideburns flicked a little pink piece of paper out of his pocket and dropped it on Gaia's tray. It had black writing on it and the only word she could make out without actually appearing to be interested was "music."

"Having a little party tonight," he said, turning sideways to let her pass. He held up his hands to give her more room. "You should show."

The irrational part of Gaia's brain couldn't believe that someone had just asked her to a party. Her.

4

Public enemy number one. The rational part of her brain formulated a sentence and sent it to her voice box.

"I'd rather sing a Barry Manilow song in front of the entire school," she said, moving past him.

Sideburns laughed. "I'll rent a karaoke machine!" he called after her.

Gaia never smiled on Mondays. But if she did, that exchange might have been worthy of one.

AS GAIA LOWERED HERSELF INTO
the chair across from Ed, he plucked a little piece of bright pink paper from her overloaded tray.

Screw Him

"Come one. Come all," Ed read aloud. "Free beer. Free music. Free love." He chuckled and placed the tiny flyer on the table between them. "Going hippy on me, Gaia?"

She lifted one shoulder as she took a swig of her soda. "Some guy gave it to me," she said, jabbing a meatball with her fork. Ed's stomach turned over, and not just because she was actually consuming a cafeteria-made meat substance.

Another guy?

More guys?

Didn't he have enough to deal with?

"Who?" Ed asked, trying to keep the psychotic jealousy out of his voice. It was still there, but if she noticed, she didn't show a sign. She just chomped on another meatball as her eyes scanned the room.

"Him," she said finally, pointing with her fork across the large cafeteria at Tim Racenello. Abercrombie boy. Skier. Former friend. Definitely charming. Damn.

"Are you going to go?" Ed asked, pushing his chicken noodle soup sans chicken—a cafeteria specialty—around with his spoon. *Please say you're not going to go. Please say you're not going to go.*

"Ed. Come on. No," she said.

Cool.

"I was kind of thinking about going to see Sam tonight," she said, actually sounding tentative. "You know, find out . . . if there's anything to find out."

Not cool.

"Well, I'll go if you'll go," Ed offered, putting his spoon down and laying his hands flat on the table. The action helped to keep him from sinking into the bottomless black pit that had opened beneath his chair at the sound of Sam's name. Amazing. It was just one little syllable. Sam. More like a grunt than a name.

Yet it held so much power.

"Go where?" Gaia asked, confused. Ed felt his

delirious mind step off its rambling path and snap into the now. He wondered if she thought he was offering to go to Sam's with her. Not likely.

"The party," Ed said, forcing a smirk. "Focus, G."

Gaia froze with a forkful of mashed potatoes halfway into her mouth. It took her a couple of seconds to decide whether to eat or talk. She did both.

"You want to go to this thing," she said as soon as she'd swallowed. Statement. Disbelieving statement. When had he lost the moniker of Ed "Shred" Fargo, party animal? As if he really had to ask that question.

"Tim's pretty cool," Ed told her. He hoped against hope she would go against every fiber of her being and agree to go with him. "We used to hang out before my hanging involved the chair."

Gaia's gaze flicked in Tim's direction. "He stopped hanging out with you after . . ." She let the sentence trail off, probably because she still didn't know how Ed had ended up without leg power.

"No," Ed answered the unfinished question. "I stopped hanging out with him. I stopped hanging out with a lot of people." He immediately felt his spirits start to wane. He was coming dangerously close to losing the nonchalant thing he'd gone to great lengths to develop. Clearing his throat, Ed pushed all melancholy thoughts aside. He'd rejoined the social world a long time ago. There was no need to dwell on the dark past. The now demanded his full attention.

"So are you going to go with me or not?" Ed asked, downing a spoonful of his now cold soup. Somehow it tasted better cold. Took the edge off.

"I don't know, Ed. . . ."

She was thinking of Sam. He knew it. He could tell by the regretful little cloud in her eyes. Like she was thinking of him and ashamed of herself for thinking of him. There was only one way to make Gaia agree to party with him. The one way he could get Gaia to do almost anything. Get her angry. Or at least righteously indignant.

"Sam hasn't called, has he?" Ed asked, feeling like the soap scum wad in the corner of his shower. The one with the black mildew gathering on it.

Her eyes flashed. Score one for the soap scum. "No," she said flatly.

"Then why are you planning on going over there?" Ed asked casually, pushing his tray away. It hit Gaia's and moved it an inch over the lip of the table toward her.

"I'm not," she said, pushing her own tray back. Ed's went two and a half inches off the end. At least. It was almost too easy. And it made him feel almost too guilty. Almost.

"Then go to the party," Ed said, pushing their trays back so that they were centered evenly on the table. He laced his fingers together and rested his elbows on the arms of his wheelchair. "Screw him."

Gaia blinked. Ed could practically see the little consonants and vowels that made up his words sinking into her brain.

"Fine," she said. "Let's go."

HE WAS IN HER ENGLISH CLASS.

How convenient. She'd never noticed him before, but there he was. Front row, window seat. Good view and a fast escape route. And he was eating a Hostess cupcake. That was comforting. At least he had good taste in food.

Gaia made her way across the room, her battered sneakers squeaking loudly on the linoleum floor. He didn't see her and she didn't exactly have an opening line, so she dropped the bag she was carrying on his desk with a half flop, half clatter.

First ever Monday smile

If he was startled, he hid it well. He chewed, swallowed, and looked up. His eyebrows arched when he saw her, but he recovered quickly and leaned back in his chair, smiling up at her. He had chocolate stuck to his two front teeth.

"If it isn't Gaia the Brave," he said, running his tongue quickly along his bottom teeth to clear the sugary goo. It didn't help the top portion of his mouth, but Gaia wasn't about to point that out.

"Got another one?" she asked, pushing a strand of hair behind her ear. It fell right back into place and she didn't touch it again. Pointless. As were all attempts at grooming in Gaia's book.

Sideburns Tim experienced momentary confusion marked by a quick squint of the eyes. "Another what?"

"Cupcake," Gaia said, shifting her feet. That was when she noticed that Heather Gannis was sitting two rows behind Sideburns Tim, shooting Gaia a glare that was now so familiar to her, Gaia could probably have mimicked it in her sleep. She looked Heather directly in the eye and spoke to Tim. "If you give me a cupcake, I'll come to your little party."

Heather visibly paled. Even her normally lined lips were white. It was all Gaia could do to keep from breaking the no smiling on Mondays rule. It was an odd Monday when that almost happened twice.

Sideburns Tim pulled a single wrapped cupcake out of his bag and tossed it at Gaia. She caught it in one hand without even flinching.

"I don't know if it's your lucky day or mine," he said with a smirk that displayed a small dimple just behind a very light layer of stubble. Probably sexy in some circles. In Heather's circle, from the look of pure horror on the girl's face.

"It's yours," Gaia said. His smirk deepened. She pocketed her cupcake, and walked to the back of the room, allowing herself a brief moment of pride. It had been a long time since she'd come out with a comeback line she liked on the spot, and not approximately three and a half hours later when it was useless.

The fury was coming off Heather in waves. As Gaia took her seat, she wondered if Heather had spoken to Sam this weekend. If she knew what had happened between Gaia and her beloved boyfriend. If she did know, Gaia really wished the girl would clue her in. But somehow Gaia doubted that was going to happen.

In fact, since she hadn't received any idle death threats, Gaia figured Heather was thus far clueless. Maybe even more clueless than Gaia was. Gaia, at least, knew she'd been in Sam's room. Worn Sam's clothes. Even if there had been no touching of the lips, she was sure Heather would throw a Springer-worthy psycho tantrum if she knew what Gaia knew.

Leaning back in her chair, Gaia tore open her package of chocolatey goodness and propped her knees up on the desk in front of her. Sure, Sam hadn't called. Yes, she'd just committed herself to an actual social function. Yes, she was living with a heinous shrew with a special place in her heart for slut clothes and bad perfume. Misery abounded.

But the thought that she actually knew something about Sam that Heather didn't know, was the thing that brought the first ever Monday smile to Gaia Moore's lips.

HEATHER GANNIS WAS HAVING

Sick of Everything

a very bad day, and trying to keep herself from screaming in the middle of English class wasn't making it any easier. Sam was avoiding her, her best friends had all gone out the night before without her and couldn't shut up about it, and the only reason she hadn't gone was because she had fully expected Sam to call her, which he, of course, hadn't.

She traced the pink line down the side of her paper with her pen, pushing so hard she tore a hole in the page. She was getting so sick of everything. Sick of Sam's avoidance of conflict policy. Sick of her friends who dropped money on cab rides and bars like they were a necessity. Sick, most of all, of Gaia Moore.

Mr. MacGregor sauntered into the room and immediately started passing out pop quiz papers. Lovely. What kind of person gave a quiz the day after Thanksgiving weekend? It was like the man lived to see students suffer. What next? Was her hair going to start falling out in clumps?

Heather adjusted the collar on her itchy wool sweater and pushed her thick brown mane back behind her shoulders. Whatever she did, she couldn't let her misery show. She needed to constantly keep the three C's in high gear. Cool, calm, collected. Otherwise there would be questions from her legion of followers. And questions, at this point, were something she couldn't handle.

Missy Ryan handed the quiz papers back and Heather took one and passed the stack along. Nothing on the page looked remotely familiar. Her body temperature skyrocketed. Heather turned the paper over with a slap and took a long breath. She had to chill. Now.

She hazarded a glance over her shoulder at Gaia. She, of course, was busily scratching away at her paper, oblivious to the world around her. The girl practically looked happy. That never happened. Something in the cosmic balance of Heather's universe had shifted, and she didn't like it.

Tim asking Gaia to tonight's party was the last straw. Heather faced forward again and twisted a lock of hair around her finger violently, yanking at her scalp. The only thing that had kept Heather going this weekend was looking forward to tonight's little shindig. She'd talked it up to all her friends, making sure they would all be there. There was nothing better than a free party with free dancing and free alcohol, even when her boyfriend was `freakishly AWOL`.

But a party with Gaia Moore present was another story.

A party with Gaia Moore present was something to avoid at all costs. Unless it was a wake and Gaia was the guest of honor.

From: smoon@alloymail.com
To: gaia13@alloymail.com
Time: 2:48 P.M.
Re: Thanksgiving

Gaia,

Thanks for an . . . interesting Thanksgiving. I'll never forget it. I want to see you, but I have finals right now and I really have to concentrate on that. Can I call you when I'm done?

—Sam

<<SEND>>

Normally, I don't go in with a plan. I never know who I'm going to want until I'm in the moment. I do have a special place in my heart for brunettes, though. They often think they're ordinary. Plain. Not sexy. They act like they have something to prove. And that always makes things more interesting.

But I'm not averse to the occasional blonde. Redhead. Asian, African-American, Indian, Latina, etc., etc. I'm not averse to anything. Like I said, it depends how I feel in the moment.

Tonight, however, I have a plan. Two, actually. One brunette. One blonde. Maybe neither will resist. But hopefully at least one of them will.

It's the breaking-down process that makes for riveting reading.

"Come on, Gaia," Ella said, placing her napkin on the table. **ready** She was all **and** glee. "Tell **willing** George about your little Sam."

EVEN AFTER HEATHER. EVEN

Ella's Salvation

after Marco. After David. After her father. After every deranged, psychotic, evil, slimy, grime-covered, bad-cologne-wearing, midnight assailant. Even after dealing with each and every one of these hateful beings, Gaia could quite honestly say she had never felt so much rage before in her life.

And from the look on Ella Niven's face, the woman was just smart enough to know that this rage was directed at her.

"You lied to me," Gaia said. There was no surprise in her voice. Only the rage. Ella's face went white for a moment underneath her layers of foundation and powder. She backed away from the foul-smelling sludge she was frying into a black pulp on the stove, and crossed her arms over her chest. Gaia wondered if Ella was remembering when Gaia punched her. Remembering and fearing.

God, she hoped she was.

"I don't appreciate your tone, Gaia," Ella said, wiping her hands on her ruffled apron. Gaia was surprised the woman even knew what an apron was. Or a kitchen for that matter.

"I was with someone on Thanksgiving," Gaia said, trying desperately to ignore the burning, acrid stench

19

that was assailing her nostrils and choking her airways. Her eyes were watering, and she suddenly registered the fact that Ella was actually cooking—or attempting an unreasonable facsimile thereof. She never cooked. Was this just another facet of the torture she had to endure?

Ella took a deep breath—how she managed it Gaia had no idea—and smoothed her blazing red hair behind her shoulders. "And how, exactly, does that make me a liar?"

The disturbing image of Gaia grabbing Ella by the back of the head, slamming her face into the frying pan and holding it there flashed through Gaia's mind. Tempting, but not an option. For the moment anyway.

"You told me there was no one there, at the hospital," Gaia said, leaning into the counter in front of her, her veins throbbing in her forehead. To think there was a time when she'd felt badly for laying Ella out. When she'd regretted punching the woman so hard her knuckles hurt. She only wished she'd done more.

Ella's amphibian green eyes narrowed into angry slits. "That's right," she said calmly. "There was no one with you at the hospital. God only knows what you did before then. I did tell you they found you outside some dorm babbling about someone named Sam." She ran her fingernail along the side of her mouth, reminding Gaia of a cat who'd just finished off the forbidden goldfish. "Is that who you're talking about?" she said with a light laugh. "Maybe he'd just kicked you out of his room."

There was a moment without air. No intake whatsoever. A moment when Gaia's heart felt as if it was about to burst open from the pressure.

Her first inclination was to launch herself at Ella and make her take it back.

Her second inclination was to entertain the idea that she might be right.

That was the standard Gaia-as-masochist inclination.

But no. It wasn't possible. Sam had said thanks. He'd said he wanted to see her again. She was no relationship expert, but if he'd booted her, he wouldn't be saying that. Right?

And he wouldn't have left her outside in the cold, bruised and woozy and half comatose.

Not Sam.

Gaia rounded the counter and in one long stride, got within centimeters of Ella's pointy little face. She was quite satisfied by the rather large jump on Ella's part.

"I swear to you Ella, if you don't tell me the truth right now—"

There was a door slam, and two pairs of eyes darted to the kitchen entry.

"George," Ella whispered, sounding as if she was uttering the name of salvation.

"I'm home!" George shouted from the foyer. "What smells so interesting?"

Gaia felt her muscles untighten and she pulled away reluctantly. The threats were going to have to wait for another day, unless she wanted to explain to George why she'd kicked his wife's scrawny ass as his homecoming present.

Buffy the Vampire Slayer™

"Well, we could grind our
enemies into powder with a
sledgehammer, but gosh,
we did that last night."

—Xander

As long as there have been vampires,
there has been the Slayer. One girl
in all the world, to find them where
they gather and to stop the spread of
their evil and the swell of their numbers.

LOOK FOR A NEW TITLE
EVERY MONTH!

Based on the hit TV series created by
Joss Whedon

Everyone's got his demons....

ANGEL™

If it takes an eternity, he will make amends.

❖

Original stories based
on the TV show
Created by Joss Whedon
& David Greenwalt

Available from Pocket Pulse
Published by Pocket Books

2311-01